Animal Person

ALSO BY ALEXANDER MacLEOD

Light Lifting

Animal Person

ALEXANDER MacLEOD

JONATHAN CAPE
LONDON

1 3 5 7 9 10 8 6 4 2

Jonathan Cape is part of the Penguin Random House group of companies whose addresses can be found at global.penguinrandomhouse.com.

Penguin
Random House
UK

Copyright © Alexander MacLeod 2022

'In the Waiting Room' from *Poems* by Elizabeth Bishop published by Chatto & Windus. Copyright © 2011 Alice H. Methfessel Trust. Reprinted by permission of The Random House Group Limited.

'In the Fall' from *Island* by Alistair MacLeod published by Vintage. Copyright © Alistair MacLeod 1976, 1986, 2000. Reprinted by permission of The Random House Group Limited.

Alexander MacLeod has asserted his right to be identified as the author of this Work in accordance with the Copyright, Designs and Patents Act 1988

First published by Jonathan Cape in 2022

penguin.co.uk/vintage

A CIP catalogue record for this book is available from the British Library

ISBN 9781787332867

Printed and bound in Great Britain by Clays Ltd, Elcograf S.p.A.

The authorised representative in the EEA is Penguin Random House Ireland, Morrison Chambers, 32 Nassau Street, Dublin D02 YH68

Penguin Random House is committed to a sustainable future for our business, our readers and our planet. This book is made from Forest Stewardship Council® certified paper.

For my mom and dad, Anita and Alistair.

*I stop and turn my face from the wind and look back the
way I have come. My parents are there, blown together
behind me. They are not moving, either, only trying to hold
their place. They have turned sideways to the wind and are
facing and leaning into each other with their shoulders
touching, like the end-timbers of a gabled roof.*

ALISTAIR MACLEOD,
"In the Fall"

But I felt: you are an *I*,
you are an *Elizabeth*,
you are one of *them*.
Why should you be one, too?
I scarcely dared to look
to see what it was I was.

ELIZABETH BISHOP,
"In the Waiting Room"

CONTENTS

Animal Person

LAGOMORPH

SOME NIGHTS, WHEN THE RABBIT AND I ARE BOTH down on the floor playing tug-of-war with his toy carrot, he will suddenly freeze in one position and stop everything, as if a great breakthrough has finally arrived. He'll look over at me and there will be a shift, his quick glance steadying into a hard stare. I can't escape when he does this and I have to look back. He has these albino eyes that go from a washed-out bloody pink ring on the outside through a middle layer of slushy grey before they dump you down into this dark, dark red centre. I don't know, but sometimes when he closes in on me like that and I'm gazing down into those circles inside of circles inside of circles, I lose my way, and I feel like I am falling through an alien solar system of lost orbits rotating around a collapsing, burning sun.

Our rabbit—my rabbit now, I guess—he and I are wrapped up in something I don't completely understand. Even when I imagine that I am reading him correctly, I know that he is reading me at the same time—and doing a better job of it—picking up on all my subconscious cues and even the faintest signals I do not realize I am sending out. It's complicated, this back-and-forth. Maybe we have been spending a little too much time together lately. Maybe I have been spending a little too much time thinking about rabbits.

As a species, let me tell you, they are fickle, stubborn creatures, obsessive and moody, quick to anger, utterly unpredictable and mysterious. Unnervingly silent, too. But they make interesting company. You just have to be patient and pay close attention and try hard to find the significance in what very well could be their most insignificant movements. Sometimes it's obvious. If a rabbit loves you or if it thinks you are the scum of the earth, you will catch that right away, but there is a lot between those extremes—everything else is in between—and you can never be sure where you stand relative to a rabbit. You could be down there looking at an animal in grave distress, a fellow being in pain, or, almost as easily, you might be sharing your life with just another bored thing in the universe, a completely comfortable bunny who would simply prefer if you left the room.

Most of the time, none of this matters. We carry on our separate days and our only regular conversations are little grooming sessions during which I give him a good scratch between the ears, deep into that spot he cannot reach by himself, and in return he licks my fingers or the back of my hand or the salt from my face.

But today is different. Today we have crossed over into new, more perilous territory and, for maybe just the next five minutes, we need a better, more reliable connection. For that to happen, he will have to do something he has never done before: move against his own nature and produce at least one clear sound with one clear purpose behind it. I need this rabbit to find words, or whatever might stand in for words. I need him to speak, right now, and tell me exactly what the hell is happening.

—

It is important to establish, before this begins, that I never thought of myself as an animal person. And since I do not come from a pet family, I never thought the family we were raising needed any more life running through it. Especially not a scurrying kind of life, with its claws tap-tap-tapping on the hardwood floors.

The thing you need to understand—I guess it was the deciding factor in the end—is that my wife, Sarah, is dramatically allergic to cats. Or at least she used to be. By this I mean only that she used to be my wife and then, later on, my partner. Like everybody else, we changed with the times, and when the new word came in—probably a decade after we'd been married in a real church wedding—we were glad to have it. We felt like a "partnership" described our situation better, more accurately, and, to be honest, we'd never really known how anybody was supposed to go around being a wife or a husband all the time.

But I'm not sure what terminology you could use to describe what we are now. "Amicably separated," maybe, or "taking a break," but not divorced, not there yet. The legal system has not been called in. Sarah and I are not ex-partners. We still talk on the phone almost every day and we try to keep up with the news of everybody else, but it has already been more than a year and I have never been to her new place in Toronto, the condo on the thirty-fourth floor.

I can imagine her there though, going through the regular Saturday-morning routine. It is probably pretty much the same as it used to be. I see her walking from one room to the next and she has a magazine or her phone in one hand and a cup of tea in the other. She looks out a high window, maybe she contemplates traffic. I don't know. Really, she could be doing anything with anybody. Every possibility is available to her, just as it is for me, and only a few things are non-negotiable anymore. Like the allergy. Unless there has been a medical procedure I'm not aware of, then wherever she is and whatever she's doing, Sarah remains, almost certainly, allergic to cats. Her condition is medically significant, EpiPen serious, so that option was never there for us. And even the thought of a dog, a dog with its everyday outside demands—the walks and the ball-throwing and the fur and the drool and the poop bags in the park—that was always going to be too much, too public, for me.

If we had stayed like we were at the start, if it had been just the two of us all the way through, I think we might have been able to carry on forever and nothing would have happened. The problem was our children, three of them, all clustered in there between the ages of seven and thirteen. They were still kids at this time. It was the moment just before they made the turn into what they are now.

When I look back, I see this was the peak of our intensity together, a wilder period than even the sleepless newborn nights or the toilet training, and I don't know how we survived for years on nothing but rude endurance. It was probably something automatic, the natural outcome of great forces working through us. We were like a complicated rainforest ecosystem, full of winding tendrils, lush, surging life, and steaming wet rot. The balance was intricate and precise and we were completely mixed up in each other's lives, more fully integrated than we would ever be again.

The kids had been pushing and pushing us and eventually we just gave in. All the friends had animals, all the neighbours and the cousins. There were designer wiener dogs and husky pups with two different-coloured eyes and hairless purebred cats. It felt like there was no way to escape the coming of this creature.

We started with the standard bargain aquarium set-up and a cheap tank bubbled in our living room for about a month while we drowned a dozen fish in there. After that, there was brief talk about other possibilities, but in the end, the rabbit felt like our best option, a gateway to the mammal kingdom. Better than a bird or a lizard, we agreed, more personality, more interaction.

"Maybe a rabbit is almost like a cat." I remember saying those words.

We got him from a Kijiji ad—"Rabbit available to a good home"—and the Acadian man who once owned him ended up giving him to us for free.

I went to his house and visited his carpeted basement. I learned all about the food and the poop and the shedding.

"Is there anything special we need to do?" I asked. "We don't have any experience."

"You just don't eat the guy," the man said. "Rabbits are right there, you know, right on that line." He made a karate-chopping motion, his hand slicing down through the air. "You either want to be friends with them or you want to kill them and eat them for your supper. We had two other people come here already today. And I was going to take the ad down if you were the same as those bastards. I could see it in their eyes, both them guys. I could just tell. They'd have taken him home and probably thrown him in a stew, a fricot, like my grand-mère used to make, you know? Hard to look at, I tell you, when somebody's lying to your face like that."

I asked him what he saw when he looked in my eyes. He laughed and bonked his temple with his finger. "I got no clue," he said. "All we can ever do is guess, right? No way to ever be sure about what's going on up there. But me, thinking about you right now? Me, I'm guessing that you are not the guy who is going to kill our Gunther."

"Gunther?" I said.

He crouched down and said the word three times very quickly and he made a clicking noise with his tongue.

The rabbit came flying out from beneath the sofa and went over to the man and stretched up to get his scratch between the ears.

"He knows his name?"

"Of course he does. Doesn't everybody know their own name?"

"And do we have to keep that one?"

"You do whatever you want, my friend. After you leave here, he's going to be your rabbit. But if you want him to know when you're talking to him, I think you better call him what he's always been called."

I stretched out my hand and Gunther sniffed at my fingers, then gave me a quick lick. His tongue seemed so strange to me then. So long and dry. The tongue of a rabbit is very long and very dry.

The man smiled.

"That there is a very good sign," he said. "Doesn't usually happen like that. Gunther, he is usually shy around new people. Normally takes him a little while to make up his mind."

The rabbit pushed his skull against my shin, scratching an itchy part of his head on the hard bone running down the front of my leg.

I felt the change coming.

"So we have a deal, then?" the man said.

"I think so," I said. And we shook hands.

"And you're promising me you will not kill him?" He half laughed that part at me.

"Yep," I said, and I shook my head. It was all ridiculous.

"But maybe you can say the real words to me, right now, out loud?"

There was no joke the second time. He looked at me hard and I stared back. He had not yet let go of my hand and as we were standing there, I felt the little extra compression he put around my knuckles, the way he pushed my bones together.

"I promise I will not kill Gunther."

"That is very good," the man said, and he smiled and then he shrugged. "Or at least, I guess that is good enough for me."

It took maybe three weeks before Sarah and I started talking about putting him down.

"This isn't working," she said. "Right? We can both see that. Whatever happens—we try to sell him or we take him back or to a shelter or whatever, I don't care—but it cannot go on like this. It's okay to admit we made a mistake."

The kids had already lost interest and the litter box was disgusting. We were using a cheaper type of bedding and Gunther hated it. In the first couple of days he'd already shredded up two library books and chewed through half a dozen cords without ever electrocuting himself. There was an infection too, something he'd picked up in the move. Maybe we gave it to him, but it was horrible to look at. He had this thick yellow mucus matting down the fur beneath his eyes, and both his tear ducts were swollen green and red. He hardly ate anything and instead of the dry, easy-to-clean pellets of poop we'd been promised, he was incontinent. For about a week, our white couch, the couch we still have, the couch where Gunther and I still sit while we watch TV, was smeared with rabbit diarrhea.

It was getting bad for me too. Something in my breathing had started to change and a case of borderline asthma was settling deep into the membranes of my chest. I felt this moist tenderness blooming in my lungs—like a big bruise in the middle of me—and I was starting to have trouble walking up or even down the stairs in the mornings. We weren't sure of the cause yet, and it couldn't be pinned directly on Gunther. The doctors said there were other possible explanations—adult-onset conditions that could stay dormant in your body for decades before springing up fresh in your later life. I had my own wheezing theories, though, and I felt pretty certain that this rabbit and I were not meant to be together.

We took him to a veterinarian who couldn't help us at all.

The guy plunked Gunther down on the stainless-steel examination table and he shone that light into his eyes and his ears and felt around, up and down Gunther's whole body. It took less than ten minutes. Then he snapped off his purple gloves and threw them into a sterile waste basket.

"Look," he said, "I've got to be honest here." He cocked his head towards the door. On the other side, in the waiting room, there were at least ten other people, all sitting there with their leashes and their treats and their loved ones. "I think you can see, we're pretty much running a cat-and-dog shop here. You know what I mean? That's ninety-five per cent of what we do. And I'm afraid we don't have a lot of experience with the exotics."

"Exotics?" I said. "What, is a rabbit exotic now?"

"It is for me. I'm just telling you: I've given you the standard examination that comes with our basic billing package. The next step is going to be X-rays and advanced diagnostics, and I don't think you really want to go there. Not for a rabbit anyway. Not for a rabbit that hasn't even been fixed."

In that moment, it was almost over. Gunther was nearly part of our past. The way to a different version of the future, a new opening, was right there.

"Listen," he said. "How about I give you the room for a little while and maybe you can have some time to think about how you'd like to say goodbye. When I come back, if you're good with it, I can give him a little sedative that will calm everything down. Then we set up the IV and whenever you want to release the drug, that will be it. It'll all be over in a painless, quiet, peaceful way. If he can't eat and he isn't drinking and he can't see, what kind of a life is that?"

As he left the room, I watched him shifting his facial features, moving from the serious life-and-death mode he'd been using on us to the cheerful semi-annual checkup face he used for his regular clients.

I turned back to Sarah, but she was already packing Gunther up to bring him home.

"Fuck that guy," she said to me.

I smiled and nodded. My wife does not like to be bossed around by anyone.

We took Gunther home and she got to work on the computer. Online she found a woman in the country who was kind to us but no-nonsense. She was a real farm vet—herds of cattle, giant pigs, even racehorses—and she rarely worked with pets, but she sold us the antibiotics we needed for twenty-five dollars flat and she told us exactly what to do. There were teeth problems, she said. Severely overgrown teeth, looping inside Gunther's head, cutting him every time he tried to chew. The infection had started in his mouth. The other guy had never even looked in there.

"It's not pretty right now," the vet said. "And I'm not going to touch anything, but once it's cleared a little, after the medicine has worked, you're going to have to cut them back."

All of this really happened to us, to Sarah and to me. For an entire week, we fed Gunther with a plastic syringe. In our food processor, we blended up this disgusting kale smoothie with the medication mixed into it. Then I wrapped the rabbit's squirming body in a towel and held him against my chest, squeezing all four of his legs into me. His hair came out, sometimes in thick clumps, sometimes in a translucent fuzz that floated through the room and, for sure, penetrated deep into my own body. Sarah forced open his mouth and she drove tube after tube of that green sludge into him. He tried to spit it back up, but most of it went down and the rest dribbled over his chin where it later hardened into this thick green grit in his fur.

But the drugs worked and a week later, when he had his strength back, Sarah and I switched places and did as we'd been told. She held him in the towel and I took a brand-new pair of wire-cutting pliers—purchased and sterilized just for this task— and I peeled back Gunther's gums.

You could see it right away. It's easy to tell when things are almost perfectly wrong. Each of his two front teeth was a brownish-yellow tusk, like a miniature ram's horn, curved back- wards almost to a full circle with a black streak of what seemed like a blood vessel flowing inside of it. I tried to imagine how things should look if they did not look like this and I tried to summon up a picture for how a rabbit's teeth are supposed to be, although I had never seen a rabbit's tooth before.

Then I just did it. I picked a spot and I aimed the scissor point of the pliers and tried to hit it. Gunther was furious, snort- ing hard through his nose. Sarah could barely hold him, but even in that moment of crisis he could not generate anything more than a cough.

"Go!" she said. "Do it right now. Now. Come on."

I brought the cutters down on the surface of the bone and I squeezed hard and quick, but the tooth was much, much softer than I expected. There was a snap and a section an inch and a half long flew across room. The second piece, snipped from the second tooth, was a little longer, and it nearly went down his throat before I flipped it free with the tip of my own finger. I dipped my hand in and out of Gunther's mouth. But then it was done and Sarah let him go and he fled beneath the bed.

We were standing there together, Sarah with the soiled towel—Gunther had let go of everything—and me with the pliers in my hand and the chunks of rabbit teeth on the floor. I plucked a piece of fur out of her eyebrow and I remember that she put the towel down and wiped her palms down the front of her shirt, then mine.

"That was not what I expected," she said.

"Me neither," I said.

Beneath the bed, Gunther remained perfectly silent. A stranger, entering the room, would not have known he was even there, and neither of us could tell if he was in agony under the mattress or if he felt any sense of relief.

"What do we do now?" I asked.

"I don't know," she said. "I guess we wait."

—

Somehow it worked the way it was supposed to. With the medicine kicking in and his teeth fixed, Gunther returned to his regular diet of raw timothy hay. Eventually his poop hardened up and his eyes cleared. Even the kids came back to him. They played games together now, flinging his carrot across the room for fetch, and they worked up a pretty funny matador routine. If you shook a dish towel at him and shouted "Toro! Toro! Toro!" Gunther would come charging across the room and blast under the fabric. This also worked great with a pyramid of plastic cups.

As soon as you built it up, he'd come barrelling through, with real strength and purpose.

When a rabbit is truly happy, they do these insane joyful leaps where they launch their whole bodies way up into the air, so much higher than you think they can go. They twist in odd ways and kick all four of their legs at the same time. It's like one of those ecstatic convulsions you see in born-again churches when people are so moved by the Spirit they can't control their limbs. Gunther used to do that all the time after the bullfight game or the plastic pyramid. That kind of jumping is called a binky. That is the real, technical term for it: *binky*.

You can never be sure, but I think that somewhere in the blur between our decision at the vet's office and the thing with the teeth and the end of everything else, Gunther's life fit into ours and we all almost made sense. He receded into the deep background of our existence and took up his place in the daily sequence. Taking care of him became a set of regular tasks. Each week it was a different person's job to change the bedding and blast the room with the Dustbuster and make sure his water and food were topped up. Allowances were paid for this labour, and Gunther became a formal responsibility of the household, like emptying the dishwasher or taking out the garbage. When other things, new emergencies, claimed us—the year Sarah's father got sick and eventually died, or the time I was laid off for eight months, or the spring when we had to take out another loan to fix the roof and repoint the chimney and replace all the gutters—I could almost forget that Gunther lived with us. Though we shared the same space, and his presence eventually put me on regular inhalers, puffers that became automatic, I still might go an entire week without actually seeing him. We were all just barely touching and it seemed like the minivan was always running in our driveway, its rolling side door gaping for the quickest possible turnaround, like an army helicopter. Sarah or I would take one step across the threshold of the front door before we'd be clapping our hands and yelling: "Let's go! Let's go! Let's go!"

Tumbling through the van door, then into and out of traffic. Every day and every night of the week there was some other activity. Piano and swimming and soccer and music and school assemblies. In an effort to spend quality time with the kids, Sarah signed up to be a Girl Guide leader. She learned all the promises and she got the uniform and we sold cases and cases of cookies. I coached a boys' soccer team for five years, though I knew nothing about soccer in the beginning.

Then lunches. Sarah and I prepared thousands of these meals for the picky, ungrateful people we had brought into the world. Whenever I cut the crusts off a sandwich or allowed someone to return a perfectly untouched but perfectly prepared Tupperware container of sliced cucumbers and ranch dip, I wondered if I was loving a child or wrecking her for the future.

Yelling and just barely making it to the corner for the first school bus at 7:30 and the second at 7:45. Then showering and getting your hair okay and putting on real clothes and going to work and dealing with all the stupid people at work. The stupid things that every stupid person said and did.

Every morning, the morning arrived just five or six hours after we'd gone down. And every morning, when Sarah and I opened our eyes again, we were already late, already behind.

"What is today?" I'd ask, and she'd look at me and blink and stare at me like I was a stranger. Then she'd turn away or concentrate on the ceiling as if she were reading a screen, like this was the dentist's office and they had a news crawl running up there.

"Wednesday," she'd say. "Wednesday is Pizza Day. No lunches. But then violin, and the after-school thing—some meeting we're supposed to go to about cleaning up the playground—somebody has to be seen to be there. Then, if there's time after that, please God, haircuts. Please. Everybody in this whole house needs a goddamn haircut."

"Yes."

"I'm serious," she said. "You need a haircut. You look like a homeless person."

I remember once, maybe five years ago—it was at a retirement party for a lady from Sarah's work—we snuck out during the speeches and fucked in the minivan, right there, doggie-style, on the third-row Stow 'N Go bench. It was ridiculous, but also absolutely the right thing to do. There were stained popsicle sticks and food wrappers back there, headphones and Lego, even a long-lost running shoe that we were so glad to find. Sarah held it up triumphantly with one hand, even as she was unbuttoning her pants with the other. "At last!" she said. "Remind me not to forget about this when we get home." The other cars just sat there by the curb under the street lights and no pedestrians ever walked by to peer through our slightly tinted windows. Inside the van, we were rushed and awkward, but we got what we came for and still made it back in time for the cake, all re-zipped and smoothed out.

I don't know what happened to us after that. There was no single event. No dramatic explosion, no other character who wandered into our lives. I think we just wore down—gradually, inevitably—and eventually, we both decided we'd had enough and it was time to move on. There must have been something else, a pull from the inside or a signal from the outside, that compelled us in some way, but I'm not sure. Maybe we really did just outlive the possibilities of each other's bodies.

But Sarah and I: we had a good, solid run and I think we came through pretty well. Three kids is not nothing and we carried those people—we carried them from their delivery rooms to their daycares to their schools and through all their summer vacations, all the way down to the fancy dinners we hosted on the nights of their high school graduations. Then, one by one, they left our house for good and, all of us, we never lived together again. Two went to universities in different cities and one moved in with her boyfriend across town and started working at a call centre.

After they left, we were by ourselves again. Together, but by ourselves now, and only Gunther stayed. The change was harder than we expected. There was too much space now and we filled it up with everything that had always been missing. Though there was no one else around, we kept getting in each other's way. I felt like the air inside the house was thickening again, but worse now, as if a clear sludge was being slowly poured into every gap in our lives. We had to slog through it every day, and every exchange was more difficult than it needed to be. Neither of us would ever watch the other person's shows and there were arguments, real arguments, about who should have the power to decide if an overhead light should be turned off or turned on. I did not like how she chewed her food, the way she incessantly talked about other people behind their backs, her selfishness. And she did not like the way I clicked my pens, the way I was always intruding on her plans, the way I started things but never finished them. No single can of soup could serve us both.

The conditions were right when the transfer opportunity came. This was a real promotion, national-level stuff—much more money and serious work, at last—the type of thing Sarah had wanted for years. She could not afford to let it pass. "A chance like this," she said, and we both knew.

After that, we started talking, quietly at first, about "making a change" or implementing "the new plan." We worked it all out, calm and serious and sad, and then it was decided. The job led the way, but we both knew it was more than that and we were clear about what this meant when we explained it to the kids. We needed to move on and there was no pretending anymore, no fudging the truth.

"We just want you to be happy," our oldest daughter said, and the line stuck in my ear because I'd always thought it was the kind of thing parents were supposed to tell their kids, not the other way around.

We kept the show running for four more months—one last school-less September through to one last all-together Christmas—and then we made the calls in the third week of January. Like everybody else, we wanted to get through Christmas before the chatter started. It was civil and transparent and even kind.

I drove her to the airport and we really did kiss and cry in a parking spot that is reserved for kissing and for crying.

"We just have to do what we have to do," she told me.

—

I look at Gunther sometimes and I wonder if he is typical—if he is like or unlike all the others of his kind, the rest of the lagomorphs that populate this world. I wonder if he has even ever seen another rabbit or if he thinks maybe I am a rabbit, too. They are an altricial species—another word I have learned—born blind and deaf and defenceless, so he would have no memory of his siblings or his mother, no sight or sound to carry forward from that first phase of his life. If there is a moment in your existence when you cannot survive without another's timely intervention—if you are like a hatchling bird fresh out of the shell—then you are altricial. When Gunther was born, he would have been a hairless three inches of flesh, a pink wriggling tube in the world, barely more than a mouth and a fragile circulatory system visible through his skin. There might have been eight or nine others with him in the litter. Maybe he still holds some faint feeling of them, the touch of other rabbits, all those teeming bodies pressed up against each other, huddling for heat. That's another word I like: the verb *to teem*. You hardly ever get to use it.

There is so much out there. I have scrolled the images on the internet and read the articles and followed the diagrams, the maps that show us what really happens if we follow them down the hole, through the warren and into the complex society they build down there, three feet beneath the place where we live. The largest and most complicated colonies can twist through hundreds of metres of tunnels and switchbacks, a path no predator could ever follow. Guided only by instinct, they dig dark mazes out of the ground, building their real working routes so that they run right beside a series of faked dead ends and false starts. Then they put in dozens of different entrances and escapes, some of them real, some of them decoys. The strategy is amazing, the fact that this level of deception, such advanced trickery, is built right into the great natural plan.

Despite all of this, in the wild, a rabbit gets to live for a year, maybe two. Less than ten per cent of them ever see that second summer or winter. I guess they are born for dying, a new generation every thirty-one days. But that's not how it is for Gunther. He is fifteen years old now, at least, and I suppose this makes him a nearly unique organism in the history of the world. From here on in, every one of his experiences will be unprecedented.

Today I decided I would try to show him something new. He has always been an indoor pet—a house rabbit—but this morning I took him outside. There was work I'd been neglecting in the yard and it had to be done. I did not think he would run away— our fences go straight to the ground—but there are gaps that are large enough and I wanted to at least give him a choice.

I put him down on the lawn and gave him a good scratch between his ears.

"There you go," I said, and I spread my arms wide as if I was granting the yard to him. "All yours."

He stared up at me, less enthused than I expected, and then he just lowered his head and pulled up a mouthful of fresh clover and started munching away. He casually turned and hopped a few feet over to sniff at the base of the back porch, near the spot where we keep our compost bin and the garden hose. He did not seem to be in a rush to go anywhere.

I turned away from him and walked towards the shed. I spun the combination on the padlock, opened the door, and wheeled out our dusty push lawnmower. I grabbed the snips and the hedge clippers and the sturdy old garden rake with its rectangular grin of sharp tines. I took out the wheelbarrow. For half an hour I purposefully did not look back in the direction where I had left Gunther. I wanted to leave him alone and give him a chance to sort things out for himself.

There had been so many spring Saturdays like this in our past, so many days full of lists, with things that needed to be done and put in order. I raked the dead winter leaves into a pile and I uncovered the beds and I took an initial stab at trimming back the rose bush and the other perennials that Sarah had always kept up. I tried to remember everything she had told me about how to get the angle right on your snips so that everything you cut away grows back and then grows out in the right way. Fullness was what we were always aiming for. We wanted the plants in our backyard to be full, to bloom thick and heavy. I touched each fork where the branches or the stems parted and I paused and thought about what to do. Then I eeny-meeny-miny-moed my way through the decisions, before cutting one side back and letting the other side live.

I turned around just in time. There was a sound, I guess, more of a vibration in the air, but it should not have been enough. I don't know what made me look. It was just a sigh, really, a gurgling exhale, like the wheezing my own lungs made at their worst, only shallower and quicker.

The thing I saw, the thing my eyes landed on, was a completely normal occurrence in the natural world, I suppose. But at the same time, it was something shocking, something completely new and troubling, to me. A snake, much thicker and much longer than the sort of animal I believed could live beneath our porch, was spiralled around Gunther's body. The drama was almost over and everything had already shifted to stillness. Gunther was stretched out to his full length and the sound coming from him, the vibration, was the last of his air being squeezed out of his body. The snake had wound round him four or five times, and their heads, Gunther's and the snake's, were touching. It seemed almost like they were peering into each other's eyes. Their tails, too, were almost even, but in between—beneath and inside the symmetry of the snake—there was this wretched contortion in Gunther's body, a twisting that seemed to spin his neck in the opposite direction from his front paws. I felt, for sure, that all his bones had already been broken.

I have looked it up—I went immediately to the computer when I came back in the house—and I know now that this other creature, the thing that once lived beneath our porch, was a rat snake, a non-venomous constrictor, as local to this part of the world, perhaps even more local, than my New Zealand rabbit. I have learned that rat snakes, or corn snakes, make great pets, that they are wonderful with kids, that they are the gentle hit of the reptile show that goes to visit all the schools. Children love to feel them spiralling around their limbs, the dry, wet sensation of it. The rat snake in my backyard was not at fault, not doing anything wrong. Only taking up its assigned place and following an instinctive pattern it could not choose or change. Gunther too was where he was supposed to be, I guess. When all of this happened, I was the only thing moving out of order. But I could not stop myself from moving.

"No," I said, and I took four or five purposeful strides towards them. Then I reached out and I picked up this strange and seething combination of whatever it was and I held it in my hand. I don't think I will ever touch anything like that again. It wasn't heavy. The two of them together did not weigh as much as a bag of groceries. They were in my left hand and, with my right, I grabbed the snake just behind its head and tried to twist it away, to pry it off Gunther and separate them. It turned on me almost instantly, unspooling from Gunther and swivelling onto my arm. I flung both of them back on the ground. Gunther fell and did not move, but the snake immediately began to head towards the pile of leaves, sideways and forward at the same time.

But we were not done yet. I grabbed the rake and followed behind, and when my chance came, I swung the tool with whatever strength I had. It arched over my shoulder and cut down quickly through the air and I felt the resistance as the point of one, maybe two of the teeth penetrated the snake's body almost in the middle. The rake descended all the way through and dug into the ground on the other side. Both ends of the snake, the top and the bottom, kept going, zigzagging furiously, but the middle was pinned down and stationary. I walked to the head, and I waited and watched the swaying. Then I timed it right and I positioned my heel as precisely as I could. I was only wearing running shoes, but I pressed down slowly, directly, and I felt the bones crushing and the liquid giving way. Like stepping on an orange, maybe. But after fifteen seconds, the swaying stopped, the top half of the snake first and then the bottom. I turned back to where I had been just a few seconds before and I was prepared for what I expected to see—the crumpled white pile, unbreathing—but it was not there. Instead, over to the side, maybe two feet away from where he had fallen, Gunther was up and at least partially reinflated back to his regular rounded shape. He was perfectly stationary now, still in the way that only a rabbit can be still, and he was staring at me, staring hard at this scene.

I looked at him and then down at the snake, the length of it, the stretch of its body. The things it had done and the things I had done. I did not know what any of them meant. I did not know what could or could not be justified. I only knew what had happened and that, eventually, I would have to come back here, to this spot, and clean up the mess. I went over to Gunther and I picked him up as gently as I could, but he gave me no reaction. He was only a soft object in my hands, almost like a stuffed animal, like a kid's toy that is supposed to stand in for a real rabbit, or for whatever a rabbit is supposed to mean. I brought him back inside, back to our house, where we are now, and I put him on the couch and knelt in front of him. I ran my fingers all along his body, like the uncaring veterinarian from years ago, but like him, I couldn't feel anything out of place, and couldn't tell if there was something else wrong, something broken deeper inside of him.

The phone rings and it is Sarah. She lives in a city where it is an hour earlier than it is here, and, for a second, I get confused about time zones and I imagine that none of this has happened to her yet.

"How you doing today?" she says.

The tone is light and easy and intimate. When conditions are right, we can fall right back into who we were. She just wants to chat about nothing, to fill in the time on an empty Saturday morning. It is quiet on both ends and I feel certain that we are both alone, at least for now.

"Well," I say. It is hard to find the right words. "Something bad happened with Gunther just now."

"No," she says, and the turn comes right away, a panicked edge sharpening her voice. "What happened?" she asks. "Is it bad? I was just thinking about him and wondering about the two of you. Is he going to be okay? Are you okay?"

"It was a snake," I say, trying to make all of this as basic as I can. "Can you believe that? Like a real snake, a pretty big one, in our yard, and it almost had him, but then he got away. I'm just not sure what's going on with him right now. Maybe he's in shock."

I make the clicking noise with my tongue and I say the name, the word that once seemed so foreign to me. I say "Gunther" and I wait for him to come but nothing happens.

The phone is pushed against my ear and Sarah's breathing is there. "Tell me exactly what happened," she instructs. "And tell me what he looks like right now. Try to explain it to me. I need details. Maybe we need to call someone."

"He seems alert," I say, "but he's not moving."

I reach out and stroke the bridge of his nose with my index finger and I feel him nudging back a little bit, trying to meet my skin with his body.

I watch this happening, almost like an extreme close-up running in slow motion, a picture that I am in and observing at the same time—my finger on his nose and his nose against my finger. There is a pause during which nothing happens. Nothing happens and nothing happens, but it goes on for too long and the gap gets too wide. I lose track.

Sarah breaks the silence.

"David!" she shouts. "David, are you there?"

My name surprises me, like an odd noise coming from another room, something crashing, and at first I don't know how to respond, but before I can do anything, Gunther twists his head, hard and quick, pivoting both ears towards me and the telephone. He recognizes Sarah's voice, the sounds that only she can make—a cry coming out of this plastic receiver, cutting through. His expression, the shape of his face, the tilt of his head, rearranges into something I have never seen before, flaccid and seized in all the wrong places. But his breathing is strong and steady. I feel like he needs me, like I am the only one who can pull him through.

"I'm here," I say into the phone, "but I can't talk right now. I have to let you go."

I hang up and stare at Gunther and I see myself reflected again at the red centre of his eye. The surface seems cloudier than normal, and I don't think he can process what is happening anymore, this hazy mixture of light and frequency that surrounds us, the familiar and the strange. I know he still knows me—he still knows us—and I try to look past my reflection. I imagine moving directly through the membranes and lenses of his eyes, down the nerves and all the way up into his brain. I think our shared past, our lives, are still there, held in his memory. Inside the mind of the oldest rabbit that has ever lived, we are a single thought—vivid and urgent and distinct—but then it passes and the rest is everything else.

THE DEAD WANT

SHE WOULDN'T HAVE FELT A THING.

They kept coming back to that. Once in every call, someone would say the words and the person on the other end would have to agree. She wouldn't have felt a thing. She wouldn't have felt a thing. It was the chorus, the refrain of the first six hours.

"At the very least"—Joe watched his mother repeat into the receiver—"at the very, very least, we can be grateful for that. All over in less than a second."

They had to wait almost a full day for the details to settle down and for the real story to make it through to them, three provinces away. The boyfriend was fine. Imagine—the boyfriend walked away barely touched. But Beatrice was done now, launched off the back of his ATV and gone for good. Bea: Twenty years old and finished with everything. And not one of them, nobody on this side, had ever even met the guy.

There'd been a party, some Friday-night thing with a campfire back in the woods, and the two of them and a bunch of others had been going home on their bikes, blasting down a converted rail line at three in the morning. He came around a turn and hit a bad rut in the trail or a rock or some stump, nothing special. It was the kind of thing that happens, a swerving. He went one way, rolling down the bank, still holding tight to the bike, and she flew off in the other direction, straight into the trunk of a tree at thirty-five miles an hour.

Decisions had to be made and it was hard to say anything that could stay solid for fifteen minutes. In the middle of every phone call, a beep would cut in from somewhere else and the line would go dead for a second and then come back again, but that small bit of nothing would be enough. It told them that plans were already changing, and they should probably stop talking now and wait for the new instructions to arrive.

His father would fly home. This was the only part they knew for sure. His father would leave on the next plane and get back as fast as possible. Back to Nova Scotia and the old place, the house where he'd grown up, the place his brother now owned. "Back to all of that," his mother said, and she pressed her lips together hard. The rest of them would drive through the night and everyone would meet up again on the other side.

"Joe will be fine in the dark," his father said, and Joe nodded. Then his dad spelled out the plan in ten seconds, as if you could do it just by saying it. "You cut into Côtes-des-Neiges on the way there. Pick up Bess and Regina at the seniors' building and drop them off when it's all over."

"Okay."

"But when you talk to them, make sure they know it's straight through, right? No restaurants and no motels. Gas and a quick piss and that's it. Make sure they know."

His voice had a tremble in it, like he was already exhausted, like he'd already gone all the way down and come all the way back. Joe looked at him, his father, almost fifty: balding on the top, grey on the sides, fat in the front. He did not look like somebody just starting out.

"It is going to be tight, but if the car can make it, we'll get all our people there for a couple hundred instead of a couple thousand. Then we can split it up even on the return."

They stood there, all three of them in the basement, pulling underwear and socks out of the dryer and stuffing them into their bags. His mother made him try on the blazer from his dark blue suit. He'd last worn it a year ago for a hockey banquet and he could feel it squeezing his shoulders. She pressed her nose into his armpit and sniffed.

"It'll do," she said. "No time to get it dry-cleaned and you'd have to be standing right up this close to see the colour."

Everyone had their own version of what had to be done. The price of the ticket was scandalous, and Air Canada was still requesting a notarized copy of the death certificate.

"Yes, I understand the policy," his father said, shaking his head while he pressed the phone to his ear. "I'll see what I can do."

Joe needed an extension on a paper and somebody to cover his shifts at the recreation centre. And his mother was going to have to spend all the banked time she'd been saving for Christmas. And then the dog. What were they supposed to do with the dog?

He knew what the drive would be like. Rolling and rolling through nothing. He'd take the full night shift and do both the big cities. His mother would spell him off only for a couple of good daytime hours. In Montreal, he'd have to feel his way through those dark streets and somehow remember which one of twenty identical seniors' high-rises held his great-aunts.

Those two would be ninety per cent of it. The old-person smell. It was already in his head. Under normal conditions, he couldn't stand next to Bess for five minutes without having to back away. And now hours and hours with the two of them rotting in the back seat. He'd have to breathe out the window. They'd come with huge floral suitcases and all kinds of special needs, and they'd spend the whole way down talking about all the dead people they knew, all the recently and distantly deceased relatives they shared. They'd think that he should know these people too, but the list of names, the dozens of strangers, all those vague half-connections, would mean nothing to him.

"Didn't I tell you? Didn't I tell you this would happen?" His mother inspected a wrinkled blouse and threw it back into the dirty pile.

"Everybody knew that boy came from trouble." His father almost whispered it. His suit bag was zipped and ready. He wouldn't have been able to pick the kid out of a lineup, but he was familiar with his people.

"All of them, that whole family. Nothing good has ever come from any of those houses. Roddie should have stopped it. He should have gone in there and split them up."

His father ran his hand along the low joists of their basement ceiling. A nest of hanging wires and bad ductwork and rusted cast-iron plumbing. Holes drilled straight through the six-by-sixes, random cut-outs and workarounds. Nothing up to code and no time and no money to fix it. Joe watched him trying to put his eyes anywhere else.

"But didn't I tell you, about those bikes?" his mother insisted. "When we saw the seven-year-olds driving those things in the parade with all their streamers and decorations? Sunny and everybody laughing and they're throwing candy and I told you. I remember I leaned over and I said: 'Somebody is going to die.' Well, what now? What are they going to say now? Still going to go on and on about how kids riding around on those things is good exercise?"

"But it's Roddie's fault too, right?" His father could not let it go. "He should have known, and he should have made sure that Bea never got mixed up with that crowd."

His mother flicked the switch.

"You be careful, Peter. You watch what you say. We're going to get there as fast as we can, but you better not start anything before we arrive. Roddie is going to be ruined. Think of that before you say a single word. He's going to be caved right in. I'm telling you: a parent cannot lose a child in this way. And it might not be over yet. Nobody knows. Things could still go very wrong, even more wrong than they already are."

"Would have been easier if it was a boy," his father said, though Joe was standing right there, still wearing the blazer. "You almost expect it to happen with a boy. They're in the paper every week. Getting themselves into scraps and messes and idiot drunk-driving car accidents. But not a girl. Not a girl like Bea, with her grades and her scholarships. Roddie should have known that boy was trouble and that he came from generations of trouble, and he was going to lead to trouble. He should have stopped it. He should have stopped it cold."

—

Beatrice and Joe and Joe and Beatrice. Though they lived far apart, they had always been close and the routine had been locked in for all their lives: Joe's family "coming home" and the kids spending two inseparable weeks together every year in the consistent heat of late July or early August. Nothing but beach days and barbecues and village festivals with their parades and summer concerts. His dad would pull the car into the driveway after ten or twelve hours on the road, and she would already be bursting through the screen door.

"It is *on*!" she would scream as she reached for him coming out of the back seat. "You have no idea what's coming!"

Once, when they were maybe eleven years old, his uncle bought a Slip 'N Slide from the Canadian Tire. He unfurled the plastic, a yellow strip like a highway line running down the treacherous steep hill of her front yard, and they did what they could to make it longer. Four rolls of Saran Wrap, a dozen garbage bags, and two old green tarps, all held down with tent pegs and bricks. They coated it all in dish soap and soaked it with the hose and kept the sprinkler running. Then they changed into their bathing suits, and she came out of the kitchen with a bottle of Crisco.

"We are so going to fly," she said, holding the cooking oil above her head. Her eyes flashed with a fierce extra light.

He was used to this with Bea, the pushing. They were born six weeks apart and they had no brothers and sisters. Their grandma called them her only, only children. He watched as Bea unscrewed the cap and poured the thick yellow liquid over her shoulders and across her collar bones. She rubbed the stuff down her elbows, then filled her palms and smeared the front of her suit and her thighs and shins. Before she handed him the bottle, she dabbed her forehead and cheeks, then took his hand and slid it over her shoulder.

"You feel that?" she asked. "It's like I'm not even here." She tried to snap her fingers in front of his face, but there was no friction and no sound. "Come on now," she said. "Your turn. Hurry up."

He lathered the grease across his bare chest and the front of his shorts and his knees and thighs. It felt hot and syrupy against his skin and the smell, like a restaurant with a deep fryer, seemed to coat the inside of his nose. He was sure it would take a week before he'd be able to wear normal clothes again. His body would keep secreting the stuff for days, like a doughnut soaking through a napkin. He could already feel it sinking into his pores.

The moment he was done, she said, "Okay, me first," and they turned at the same time and raced for the start.

She got there just before he did, and he saw only the bottoms of her feet as she launched herself headfirst and parallel to the yellow. But then he was moving too, and the strip felt more like a tube, like they were in one of those big slides at a real water park. Her body kicked up a wake of soapy water that burned in his eyes and though he could hear her all the way down, he also felt every small stone poking up through the plastic, every bump in sixty feet of hayfield pretending to be a lawn. When they hit the Saran Wrap and the garbage bags, it felt like there was nothing there at all, as if his body was sliding straight over gravel. And then there really was nothing. The hill was so steep, and they were going so fast, that even when they cleared the tarps, they kept going for maybe another ten seconds.

Her momentum gave out first and they collided. He slid up the side of her, her body like a ramp, and his slick chest rubbed the back of her legs. He tried to turn, to move out of the way, but his hips brushed across hers and he flew over the top. Then they were both on their backs, nicked with small cuts and covered in oily grass, both panting.

He said the word "Amazing," and before he could make another sound, she rolled on top of him and kissed him hard on the mouth. He tasted the different salt of her skin and her sweat waiting there underneath the cooking oil and he felt a dry sunburn patch on her bottom lip. Their chests heaved up and down in the same rhythm and he put his hands out and touched her for a second with his fingers spread out separately on each of her shoulders. Then he pushed her away and rolled out.

"No," he said, and he inhaled hard. It was as though the whole outside didn't hold enough air.

"You are something else," she told him. "You know that? You are altogether something else."

She smiled and it was as if her whole body was laughing, like there were waves of radiation coming out of her and moving right through him. It took less than three seconds, and nothing followed. They carried on as though this thing that had just happened hadn't happened at all. For another nine years, they carried on as if it might be possible, if you really wanted, to reset your past and begin again.

The Slip 'N Slide waited. Its rubbery skin stretched down the hill, beading with water, and it could not be resisted. The hose kept running and they went down at least fifty more times, trying it all the different ways. Sitting down or standing up like surfers, or switching at the midpoint and rolling front to back or back to front. You could do a somersault start or a somersault dismount, or you could pair them together. They kept it up for maybe an hour and a half before her parents called them in for something to eat. When they walked into the house, his mother saw the scratches and the oily froth, a mix of sunscreen and Crisco and nicked blood. She reached out to touch Bea's elbow, the white residue in the crease, and she rubbed her thumb and her middle finger together, then sniffed and turned away. The expression on her face and the smell hanging in the air.

"What in the name of God," she asked, "have you two been doing?"

—

For the last hundred miles, ever since Truro, the stiffness had been inching up his back, one vertebra at a time, to the base of his skull. Coffee wrenched in his stomach and buzzed in his head, and a pins-and-needles sting ran down his right leg every time he moved his foot from the gas to the brake. Twenty-six hours in the car. He'd watched the light fade to a dense purple and kept going until the morning came back again, pale at the edges at first, then burning his eyes. He felt like he was orbiting the planet, driving backwards against the sun. After Toronto, he'd started measuring the distance in tanks, filling them up and running them dry, and filling them up and running them dry. He thought he could see the needle moving, quicker than an hour hand, always emptying. He'd had only one break, an empty stretch of New Brunswick where the new road was fast and easy, and his mother took her turn piloting them through two calm hours of trees.

The great-aunts had been quiet the whole way. Once, travelling through the dark around Cabano, he thought for sure they must be sleeping, but when he turned back to check, they were both sitting straight up and side by side, two pairs of eyes pushing through their glasses and staring straight ahead.

"You keep it going," Regina had told him. "Don't worry about us."

As he made the final turn at the driveway and started up the hill, he noticed the black trees and the white sky forcing itself into the spaces left behind by the leaves. This was all new to him, the place in November, the late fall. He had never seen the house looking like what it really was: boards and shingles standing in the middle of a hard and crusted field. In the summer, the green was so thick you couldn't see anything from the road, and during all his visits, it seemed that no amount of work could ever keep up with the poplars and the knotweed and the grass. Now it was all much simpler. It was as though the trees had already moved on to the next stage. He saw them like jumbled kindling waiting for the stove.

He put the car in park, blew out a whole breath, twisted the key to off, and turned to his mother. She had the passenger mirror flipped down and was trying to press away the puffiness from beneath her eyes. She put on lipstick that was too red.

"Good driving," she said, and she reached over to squeeze his arm. "Such good driving, Joe." Then she tapped the glass of the passenger window and peered over at the house. "But this is where it really starts. We'll know pretty soon how the rest is going to go."

The side door opened, and his aunt and uncle came down to meet them, followed by his father and other relatives. His uncle was thinner than he remembered, and he walked tilted hard to the right, as if one leg were much shorter than the other.

Aunt Regina opened the door and placed one flat shoe on the gravel and then the next. When she shifted her weight to pull herself out, she groaned a bit, and he heard a faint farting noise come out of her. She stared at him.

"What?" she said, almost smiling. "That never happens to you?"

The car people and the house people met in the middle of the driveway and they exchanged their handshakes and hugs. His aunt Caroline went to his mother and they tried to hold each other though neither of them knew where to put their hands.

"We have so much food," his aunt said. "You won't believe the pile of food the neighbours brought."

"That's wonderful," his mother replied. "So nice. Isn't it a miracle how everybody comes together?"

Joe glanced at the two of them, standing in the shadow of the house, and he thought about the way his parents talked about Aunt Caroline behind her back, how they made fun of her voice and her horrible baking and her bad haircuts, and how she pronounced the word *library* like *lie-berry*. It didn't seem right that she should have to be stuck with these people right now. He felt something for her then. For the first time in all of this, he felt something, but it wasn't sadness. He stared at them again: his aunt crying quietly on his mother's shoulder and his mother placing her hand on her sister-in-law's back. He tried to pretend he didn't know them at all, tried to imagine them as strangers, his aunt just a woman in a photograph from the newspaper, the still image of a mother who had just lost her child. It was easier that way.

He shook hands with his father first and then his uncle and he could tell, just from the way those two walked and the way they stood next to each other, that something had happened between them last night. He couldn't read it clearly, but it was clearly there. Someone had said exactly, exactly the words he should not have said. He could imagine them talking at two in the morning, sliding casually into the topic they both wanted to avoid, and then accelerating into anger until it was impossible to get away from what they really thought.

His father and his uncle: two men standing outside, their hands in their pockets, one concentrating on his shoes, the other contemplating the sky. These two had the same parents and they'd lived in this house as kids and eaten the same food and shared a bed. They had the same fading hairline and the same dark eyes, the same patterns in their chromosomes, whatever—none of it enough. The next few days could be stuffed with sweet-and-sour meatballs and potato salad and lemon squares and rye and ginger, but these two were not going to come around, not going to rise above.

It hit him again how hard it was to be a member of a family, fused to all these other people you would never choose and never fully get away from.

He'd had the heat cranked in the car and now, standing in the driveway, he felt the wind and the edge of raw cold it carried. The invisible force pulled his jeans tight against his legs and flapped at his T-shirt. He stared up at the trees again and thought about how they'd been wiped perfectly clean by this same wind and this same cold. It was clinical. A machine couldn't have done a better job. If they'd hired a work crew to pick every one of those leaves, they wouldn't have been able to match the result.

His uncle jutted his chin at Bess and Regina and whispered: "I hope those two didn't drive you crazy."

Joe looked over at his great-aunts and tried to think of something funny to say. He wanted a little joke to put in here, a quick, easy line he could share with his uncle, but then a second passed and then another and nothing came to him. The opening closed. He shrugged his shoulders.

"They were perfectly fine," he said. "Didn't say a word the entire time."

—

His family had given up on religion years ago, but that didn't matter. Other people kept dragging you back into churches and temples, mosques and synagogues, and you could never escape completely. He remembered the morning it happened, a winter Sunday. His mother was wearing her maroon bathrobe and she'd just poured herself a fresh cup of coffee. The temperature had dropped during the night and yesterday's wet slush had frozen into a thick crust of jagged ice that covered everything. They would need to chip at the car doors before they could even get to the scraper and then it would take a good twenty minutes of running the defroster at full blast before they could leave. His mother looked at the clock and then at the newspaper on the table.

"I'm done," she said, and she sat down and rubbed her hand over the middle fold, smoothing out the pages. "And not just for today, either, and not because of the ice. It's over. You two can go on if you want, but they've got all they're going to get from me."

His father nodded. "Fine by me," he said. "I'm sick of them, too." He filled his own cup and he asked her for the Sports section and that was it.

They never went back, and though there'd been some uncomfortable patches—a bar mitzvah for a kid in his school, and a big Ukrainian wedding where his father had to pay money to dance with a too-tall, too-skinny bride—it was mostly manageable. As long as they kept to themselves, it was surprising how easy it was to avoid.

Now, though, as they drove to the funeral home, the nagging questions about ritual and etiquette returned and they had to scramble to make sure they all knew how to do the right thing at the right time. He'd never been to a wake before, and his father tried to prepare him for what was going to come.

"We all stand in a line and then the people come in and we

shake their hands." He said this into the rear-view mirror and Joe nodded back to the partial reflection.

"This goes on for a couple of hours. Then there will be some praying, a rosary or something like that, and then the people will leave. Then something else, I think, something just for the family, but I'm not sure. We'll see. Just try to follow along."

The crowd surprised him. There couldn't be enough houses in the village to hold all these people. The funeral home was just a small renovated place with aluminum siding, but the mourners lined up out the door and around the corner of the building. In the lobby, as you came in, there was a kind of easel holding a cork bulletin board full of photographs, pictures of Bea at different stages of her life. He was surprised to see himself in there so often. There was a shot of the two of them holding up a pair of garter snakes, and he remembered the time they'd tried to build their matching snake habitats out of two old shoeboxes filled with grass. For food, they swatted flies off the windows and slipped the dead insects under the lids.

The biggest picture, the one in the middle, was a blown-up shot of Bea playing volleyball. She'd been a power hitter and made the provincial team and gone to the Canada Games last year. In the photograph, something from the yearbook, she was suspended high in the air with her arm cocked and ready to spike the ball. Her whole body curved into the shape of a capital C. With her knees bent and her back arched like that, it seemed almost as though her feet might be able to touch the back of her head. The ball waited, perfectly set, and on the other side of the net the opposing team's blockers closed their eyes and turned their heads away. Bea's face was steady and focused. You could see a twist of muscle stretching between her elbow and her wrist.

Everyone who came to the wake knew who he was, but he knew almost none of them. He waited in the line, and when they said, "We are sorry for your loss," he said, "Thank you."

There were so many old people.

A lady said to him: "Now, are you the one who used to play hockey? The one in Ontario who they say is going to be a doctor?"

"Yes," he said. "That's me."

"Thought so," she said. "I like to keep track. Our cousin Bess talks about you. She thinks you're altogether a great fellow."

It was strange to think of himself circulating in other people's chatter. All the teachers and the principal and even the janitor came. The guy from the garage, a woman who lived down the road. His hand hurt and he rotated his ankles every once in a while. He knew nothing like this could ever happen at home. They all had different stories about Bea.

"I work at the store, and she was always so nice."

"She used to babysit our kids."

"Her mother and I are old, old friends."

He realized that everyone could do this, stop in the line and talk for thirty seconds about the little things, this or that.

"Oh," he'd say. And then, "Oh, yes," and "Thank you for coming."

He felt like he was learning something: a new set of rules, the proper technique for lobbing the ball to the other person in a conversation, nice and easy, so that both of you could get through.

It did not work like this with the younger ones. Spectacular in their grief, the kids clustered and wailed in small groups, and they came through the line laden down with teddy bears and photographs and handwritten poems. Some of them cried so loudly it felt theatrical and he was irritated by the whole performance. There were so many flowers in so many odd shapes and styles. The smell reminded him of a powerful laundry detergent, like something synthetic that had been designed to smell like a bunch of flowers.

Near the end of it, towards nine o'clock, a girl came through the line. He recognized her from the summers, one of Bea's good friends. When he shook her hand, she leaned in close to him and he felt her breasts squishing up against his arm. She whispered in his ear: "Find me when this is over. I need you to do something."

The words came out as an instruction, not a request. When she pulled back, he twisted his head around the room to see if anybody else had noticed. Then he looked at her again, but her face was back to a polite, public smile.

"It's Janice," she said. "You remember."

"Yeah," he said. "Of course."

They'd been stuffed into a car together, five of them in the back seat, Bea and her friends passing warm beer to each other as they drove down some dark gravel road that led to a square dance in an old parish hall. The headlights caught the dust of the road and the trees closed in around them, making it seem like they were travelling through a long tunnel together. Janice was a stranger sitting on somebody else's lap, but when Joe looked over at Bea, his cousin winked at him and shrugged her shoulders. He could feel her calculations, the way she tried so hard to make sure he was always inside the loop and nobody treated him like a tourist.

They drank a lot and the night smeared. The hall was packed with people of all ages and the room reeked of meat and old-man aftershave. A young fiddler and a fat lady piano player drove the crowd forward, dragging and then pounding through the sets. Everything moved in order: feet scuffing the ancient floor, always on the beat. He danced with Janice or he danced with Bea. They took turns leading him through the more complicated patterns of intersection where the older people and the kids wove in and out of each other's arms. Janice always wanted to go faster than everybody else and he remembered her face steady in front of him as they spun through the third figure, the rest of the crowd blurring behind her head.

Something could have happened between them that night. She was so close, and he had his hands on her waist, resting right above the loops of her jeans, and she had hers on his shoulders. There was an opening they both wanted to pass through, but then the dance ended, and they were going in opposite directions and needed to take separate rides home.

Before she left, Janice faced him and linked her fingers together behind his neck. She came in close and turned sideways like she was going to say something, but then her tongue darted out like an animal, and she quickly licked a drop of sweat from his ear lobe.

"Next time, Mr. Man, we plan this a little better, okay? I could have made arrangements if I'd only known."

"Yes," he said. "Yes. Next time we do it right."

But then he didn't see her at all last summer, and this was where they were now.

"You need to find me," she repeated. There was no joke left. "At the end, when the rest of this is finished, you come and find me."

The priest gathered them together for a prayer and everyone was quiet. The words sounded as though they came from another time, like something people might say if they were huddled around a big fire three thousand years ago. Eternal rest and perpetual light. The priest recited his lines and then everybody else gave the proper response. Joe looked around the room; even his mother and father, tapping into some lost reservoir from childhood, knew their parts. Even the smallest kids. He tried to read their lips—tried to guess at words like *salvation* or *almighty*—but he could not get the timing right.

When the prayers ended, they cleared the room and the family was left alone. Each person took a turn approaching the casket. Joe watched from behind as his aunt and uncle went up together and knelt side by side. His uncle's spinal cord seemed to liquefy and he slumped with his head turning to the side and coming to rest against the polished wood of the box. There was no sound from him. Aunt Caroline held his hand and, after a few seconds, she stood first and pulled him up and led him out of the room. His parents went next and then it was his turn.

He lowered himself onto his knees and looked at her. Bea was wearing a dress with thin straps that went over her shoulders and her hair was pulled back neatly. They'd done her makeup in a way that seemed almost normal, not trying too hard. The dress was dark green and made out of a velvety material. It made him think of a Christmas party. There was a silver necklace with a Celtic locket that rested precisely in the middle of her chest and her hands were folded together. Whatever had happened out there in the woods had been wiped away and there was no evidence of the collision, no sign of that force or speed or impact, nothing in front of him but a girl his own age with her eyes closed.

He tried to think about what he was supposed to be thinking about right now, or what he should be asking for during this praying part, the kneeling interval, but he could not come up with anything good, so he just stayed quiet and very still. He decided to count to twenty in his head before moving on.

The place emptied one person at a time and then even the priest pulled on his leather coat and went home. The man who managed the funeral parlour circled around collecting the stained styrofoam cups and dumping the dregs of old coffee and tea down the drain. He turned off the lights in the small kitchenette and went in to check the bathrooms. Joe heard him running water and spraying air freshener. This part was over.

He left with his parents, heading out to the small parking lot. There was no sign of the girl. His aunt and uncle were already in their car, pulling out of the driveway. His father nodded at his brother and gave a little wave as he reached for the door handle.

"One more day of this," he said under his breath and then he slumped into the seat and tilted his head upwards as if he needed to inspect the little on/off light and fabric that coated the roof of their car. "It's almost done."

His mother sat on the passenger side and Joe went in the back. His father turned the key and the engine came to life, but then

Janice was suddenly there, right beside the car, wearing a dressy blue coat now. Her mittened hand touched his father's window.

"What now?" his father whispered, and he pressed the button to lower the glass.

"Hello," she said. "Can I borrow this guy for a second?"

She waved at Joe and his father turned his head with a questioning expression.

"It's just we're doing this thing," Janice said. "A little thing for Bea, just ourselves, just her friends, and I know she'd want Joe to be there."

His father took his hands off the wheel.

"You're one of Kimberley's, aren't you?" Joe could feel him mapping her genealogy, placing her exactly where she belonged.

"Yes. Janice. The third one. Bea was my best friend."

"It's nice of you to think of Joe like this," his father said. There was a deep relief in his voice, as though this was what he'd always wanted, the real reason they'd kept coming back for all those years, to get back to something like this, to be included in the natural order. "You know where to drop him off, then?"

"Of course I do. Been going to that house my whole life."

"Good enough for me." He turned around and half smiled. It was the best he'd looked since the start of this. "Out you go, then."

Joe opened the door and stepped back into the cold. His mother called to him. He could tell she wasn't sure.

"Not too late, okay?" Her eyebrows came together tight, and he watched the way she looked at Janice and then back at him. The questions would have to wait. "Don't get yourself in a mess," she said. "Those are your only clothes for tomorrow."

"I'll be fine," he told her. "It's just a little while."

He stood beside Janice as the car pulled away and he saw his mother's reflected eyes staring at him from the side mirror. Janice stood perfectly still until the car passed out of sight, then her face changed and she jerked at his hand and pulled him away.

"Come on," she said. "Not much time left."

The funeral home sat on the outer edge of the village, touching the woods. Janice led him around the back and down a steep bank. He had to turn his feet sideways and cross his legs over and lean hard into the hill just to make it to the bottom.

It was a clear night with no moon but the stars hung thick like a strange fog floating above the sky. He held his open palm in front of his face and waited for his eyes to adjust. The country dark was always so much darker than the city dark. You could see every point of light in outer space, but almost nothing on the ground. He thought about ancient explorers crossing the ocean in their big wooden ships and he wondered if there were still people around today who could navigate the globe guided only by these patterns in the sky. He connected the dots of the Big Dipper and he imagined all the other pictures that were supposed to be up there if you only knew where and how to look. There were people who could show you the hunters and the animals and the gods in their chariots, but he was not one of them.

Janice took his hand again and led him towards a clump of brush beside a small brook.

"Cory."

The name came out short and crisp and serious. Joe's eyes were adjusting to the night and he felt his hearing tuning up as well. Her voice seemed to carry a long way.

"Come on now, Core, get up. He's here. We have to go right now."

There was a rustling, like a raccoon or something larger digging through garbage. A small light flickered on, and a man stood up and emerged from behind the brush. He'd been sleeping back there or at least huddling under a blanket and he couldn't quite straighten himself up to his full height. He was big and solid, and Joe thought he looked like somebody used to stooping under doorways or rubbing his head against the low ceilings of basements. He wore a baseball cap and blue hooded sweatshirt with the New York Giants logo stencilled on the front, a pair of filthy jeans, and some white high-top running shoes. His hair hung over his ears, black and matted, and there was a burst blood vessel in one of his eyes, the pupil and iris completely surrounded in red.

There was something wrong with him; Joe could see it. Not right in the head, and more than just drunk. Drugs or pills, he thought, or sick, really sick. The man swayed, barely present, rocking up onto his toes and then back onto his heels, and he couldn't control his thumbs. They kept moving up and down very fast, like he was some twitchy kid playing video games.

The ground was cold and wet, and Joe felt the moisture leaking through his one thin pair of dress socks. Behind the branches, beneath the flashlight, he saw the guy's nest: a soaked sleeping bag and a pile of takeout food wrappers and empty bottles. Three nights: that was his best guess. The condition of his clothes, this pile of waste, the cold that seemed to be shaking through him. Put all that together and it added up to three nights out here in a late Nova Scotia November.

The man held out his hand, his fingers and the shaky thumb reaching for Joe.

He said: "Please."

Joe had never heard it sound like that before, long and dragged out, like the guy had to work hard to hold his lips together and force enough air through to make the *p*-sound.

"Please, man."

The words made a thin mist in front of his face.

Sometimes you can almost perfectly recognize a person you've never met. The cold made Joe's teeth hurt and his fingers clench. For the first time in his life, he wanted to hit somebody. Not this guy necessarily, just somebody. He turned on Janice.

"So this is our little celebration? Just for her friends? This is the special thing we're 'doing for Bea'?"

"It's wasn't his fault, Joe."

Janice avoided his eyes.

"I was there," she said. "We were right behind, and we saw everything. It was nobody's fault." She pounded her fists deeper into her pockets. "He's a good guy. I swear to you, he's a good guy. I mean, not like this. This is something else now. But Bea was crazy about him. You have to know that. She loved him and they were going to leave here as soon as they could. She didn't care what anybody else thought. They had things they were going to do, plans. You should have seen him trying to bring her back. We were all out there in the middle of the night and it was all wrong. The bike is wrecked and everything's broken and it smells like gas and people are yelling, but he . . ."

Her arm reached out to him, her palm open and her fingers straining in Cory's direction, but there was no reaction and after a few seconds they closed back up and her hand dropped to her side.

"He kept it together and he stayed calm and right close, and he made sure nobody else touched her. He called 911 and he brought in the ambulance, and he tried to carry her out of there, but everybody knew it was already too late. We knew from the moment it happened."

She surged through the story, almost crying at the end, but neither he or Cory moved. It was as if Janice was describing something that had happened to other people. Joe looked at the brook, the water running.

"Why am I here, Janice? What do you want from me?"

"He can't get in," she said. "They won't let him see her. Not at the hospital, not the house, not here. And Bea's going to be in the ground by tomorrow at lunchtime."

She was not crying and she was not angry. It was all strategy now, things unfolding in order. There were actions that needed to happen.

"Your uncle has lost it, Joe. Says if he sees him, he's going to kill him. Says he'll do it with his bare hands. He went to Cory's trailer, and his aunt's, and his grandmother's, and he's been asking all around, trying to track him down. He doesn't care anymore. The police know, but nobody's doing anything. They think it will settle down. Maybe it will, but we don't have time for that."

"I still don't get this," he said. "Why me?"

She pointed up to the funeral home and he followed her hand. He saw the window, four feet off the ground, and the shadow of the man inside, moving through the rooms.

"They lock everything down at night and it has to be opened from the inside. He'll only need a minute to get through."

"No," Joe said. He did not need to think about it and he did not want to be here anymore.

"You're the only one who can do it."

Janice said it slow and flat. He could tell she'd plotted this all the way through and that he had always been part of the plan.

"If you go right now, they'll let you in. But it's got to be a family member. I already tried and they turned me away. It has to be family."

He shook his head. "No," he said. "No."

The scene was starting to whirl out of control and pull him in.

He knew he had to stay calm and move away from them as quickly as possible. He clenched and unclenched his hands and felt that familiar numbness in his toes and fingers, sensation draining from his extremities.

"I'm going to walk away now," he said. "I'm not going to say anything to anybody, but I have to go. I'm sorry."

He turned and clawed at the weeds to pull himself up. The points of his shoes dug into the freezing ground, and he tried to get enough leverage to take a step.

"Come on," Janice called after him. "You can't leave him like this. Think about it, Joe. The rest is nothing. Think about Bea. Ask yourself. Would any of this mean anything to her?"

He saw her as a girl on a slide, her eleven-year-old body drawn down the hill. Your first cousin was your father's brother's daughter, or your mother's sister's son, or any of the other options, but what did that mean to the two people on either side of the chain? He thought of the crowd, the people standing in line: teachers and janitors, the kids she babysat, volleyball players, fellow customers from the store. All of them waiting their turn to shake his hand. A wake today and a funeral tomorrow, yes, but who were the dead for and what did they want? In another twenty-four hours, he knew this would be over and he'd be back on the all-night drive, ferrying his passengers in the opposite direction. He glanced down at Cory and Janice, barely visible now, standing beside the brook in the cold and the flickering light, trying to hold their places. Who were they related to?

He crested the hill and stopped. The parking lot stretched in front of him, an expanse of cracked asphalt illuminated by a single street lamp. The light came down in a cone that drew a perfect yellow circle on the ground, a space with an inside and an outside. You could walk around and stay in the shadows, or you could move through. He stepped into the glare and looked up and studied the bulb. There must be a sensor inside, he thought, something that told the light when to switch on and off. He bit down on his tongue and rubbed it between his teeth. Everything else happened automatically: the turn and the steps towards the building, the stomping of the feet, and the clearing of the throat. This hand knocking quietly on the front door was not entirely under his control.

The man answered. He was already wearing an overcoat and pulling on his gloves. "Lucky you caught me," he smiled. "I was just on my way."

"I think I forgot something," Joe said. "Can I go back in for just a second?"

The man moved to the side and waved his arm like an usher. "There is always time for the family," he said. "I'll wait out here. Please. There is no need to hurry."

Joe walked past the photographs and entered the room again. It was only the two of them, but he did not stop or look in her direction. Instead, he crossed quickly to the back, found the window, and twisted the old-fashioned metal hasp. He set his feet hard on the floor and put all his weight against the frame and pushed. Old paint cracked at the sash and the air came through and moved the curtains, rustling the petals on the flower displays. He thought he heard a scrambling in the leaves below and a vaguely human sound, but he could not be sure.

He stepped back and stared down at this small opening he'd made, a gap in the wall. It was only three or four inches, but it was more than enough. Anything could come through here now.

He left the room, pulling some random keys from his pocket and jangling them in the air.

The man looked up and smiled at him. He had a small bucket of salt to spread over the front steps.

"Hard to keep track of it all, isn't it?"

"Yes," Joe said. "Feels like I'm always losing things."

The next few seconds would be critical, and he knew he needed to keep moving. If he could just get across the parking lot, it would be okay. If he could reach the other side of the circle before the man noticed anything out of the ordinary, then he could disappear, back into the darkness, and no one would see that he was alone, and no car waited to carry him home.

WHAT EXACTLY
DO YOU THINK YOU'RE
LOOKING AT?

———————————

[*Pasadena, 1975*]

I KNOW I AM NOT LIKE OTHER PEOPLE. AND, MOST probably, I am not at all like you. I did not come here, to Southern California, for a vacation, and I was not drawn by the heat or the palm trees or the chance to drive by the homes of the stars. The promise of a beach day in late December could not bring me across a continent, and I have no desire to stare at the body-builders or the roller skaters sliding by in their tank tops. I did not come to see the cartoon mouse made real in the world or to listen to his robots singing about how it is a small world after all. You will just have to trust me on this one. I have come and gone a long way around this globe—perhaps no one has trav-elled farther—and I believe I am uniquely qualified to tell you: It is, most definitively, not a small world.

My challenge, you see, my problem, is that the things that attract other people do not attract me. And when you are in my position, when you live the way I live, it feels like you can never escape from advertising. Other people are always trying to show me things and bring me places, but none of it—not one molecule, not a single atom—of what they have to offer has ever interested me. I think it has always been like this: for as long as the world has had people on it, there has always been a person like me. Someone who does not care for what is available and, instead, wants only to view the masterpiece that has never been displayed, or to touch the relic that should not be disturbed, and purchase the item that is not for sale.

Like the very particular, very peculiar, kind of light they have here at this time of year. It is why I come, because of the light. Its thick clarity, and the way it holds everything at once, but in perfect separation. I am not talking about the sunshine, you understand, and not that first brutal glare at the airport, the one that yanks the string in your brain and makes your pupils contract so quickly it hurts. No. I come for the everyday light, the stuff that just falls out of the sky, right around the solstice. I like to stand in it, stand under it, at twelve in the afternoon, when the days are almost at their shortest and the evening shadows reach almost to their longest. I want as much of this light as I can get at exactly the moment it is least available. If there was some way a person could stand directly in the light but outside of the heat, then that is what I would do, but the option has never been presented and there are some compromises that cannot be compromised. Believe me, I know how difficult it is to gain access to the one thing you want most without also coming into contact with the thing you most want to avoid. It takes a lot of work and careful strategy to do both at the same time. But I have experience.

Normally, there is a routine I have to follow. As soon as I step out of the airplane, I put my sunglasses on, even though I am still inside the terminal. They are a special mirrored wraparound model so that no one can see me and nothing sneaks in around the sides. I love this airport, LAX, more than all the others and sometimes I even have mail forwarded here. The address is 1 World Way and they have a person sitting in the business office who will hold your documents if there is something urgent you need to sign. It doesn't bother me that they are always, always under construction—I know it is the price of progress—and I appreciate that they were one of the first to accommodate the plane I like to travel on now, these new jumbo jet 747s with their upstairs lounges and their orange couches and the singers and the live bands that play for us all the way from one runway to the next.

When I have adjusted to the glasses and I can see again, I make my way down to the luggage carousel. Depending on the gate, it can be a long walk, and sometimes it can take twenty minutes to get there. This time around, for some sections of the journey, I ride on a series of conveyor belts they have recently built directly into the floors of the longest corridors. These belts carry us the same way they carry the bags. I hesitate before stepping onto one for the first time. I worry about timing my stride correctly so that I can transition smoothly from walking under my own power to this new mode of transportation. In the beginning, it feels disorienting, this sensation of standing up, standing still, and doing nothing, while another force, I guess a motor buried in the floor, takes me where it wants to go. You get used to it very quickly, though. I just like to know that I am in the right place and headed in the right direction. It does not bother me at all to imagine my own body as just a small object inside of a larger system, a vast network of coordinated movement. I like to think that there must be someone, a great architect, who has already made a plan for me, and for the rest of us. All we have to do is follow.

At the baggage carousel, I pick out my suitcase and I walk—now with a renewed sense of purpose and speed—to the car and the driver that wait for me. Then we move out into the traffic and the noise and the smog. We take on-ramps and exits, and often we are forced to wait for hours in the snarl. During these times, when we are almost parked on the freeway, I like to stare through my tinted windows into all the other cars that surround me, the ones on the right and the left, the one at the back. I like the way people think they are invisible inside their vehicles. I like to watch them sing or smoke or touch their own faces, feeling around for tiny blemishes. Sometimes they argue with their lovers, sometimes they kiss, sometimes they scream or try to reach around and hit their children in the back seats. Sometimes there are old people along for the ride and I imagine they are all late for their doctors' appointments. This is my favourite show, the beautiful theatre of rush hour. I could sit in it all day with my tumbler and my ice cubes slowly melting into the mixture.

But eventually we get to the hotel, and I have to check in. I go to my regular room, and I close the door and I do what I do, and the reactions occur, or they don't. You can never be sure.

This time around, though, nothing is going according to plan. And though I have followed the same routine, at least through the early stages, something unexpected has happened to lead me here on foot, way off course and deep into this crowd, so early in the morning on New Year's Day.

I cannot tell yet if this is a new possibility or just the old problem presenting itself in a new way, but I know that it feels different, and I can sense a change coming. One step is all it will take. My weight has already started to shift, and I imagine I will have to say her name as I lurch forward, and I will probably need to yell to be heard above this noise—the oboes and the saxophones and piccolos all warming up.

"Tanya, Tanya, Tanya!" I will cry out as loudly as I can. Then something else will happen. And something else after that, but for the first time in a very long time, I do not know what it will be.

—

I can already sense that this is going to be difficult to explain. The operation of forces I am talking about, so massive and temporary, here and gone, weather and money and airplanes. And it is almost impossible to demonstrate to another person. The way I see it: everything linked and all of it tied directly into the movement of the planets and our little blue-green orbit around the sun.

But it is there in the suitcases: the pattern of our travels, where we have come from and where we are going, and the little moments where we cross over. This is why I need them, you understand, all my surprise bags, the whole collection.

They do not belong to me, not in the usual sense. I did not pack them and I never know what they contain until I am safely in my room and I slowly undo the wraparound zippers or cut off the locks with my snips. I did not own them before and I do not own them now, and I never keep them longer than I need to. In my hopeful imagination, not long after I drop them off again near the lost luggage counter, they all eventually make their way home, but I understand that this period of uncertainty cannot be easy for the original people, the ones who must fill out the forms describing the outside appearance and what they remember of the contents.

I know that because of me—because of my individual desires and my individual actions, because we have intersected in this way—all the original people are experiencing a unique sense of despair at the same moment when I am most full of hope. And even as I walk away from the carousel as quickly and as purposefully as I can—the anticipatory energy pulsing in all my cells—I know that they are just at the start of their long and disappointing delay. Most likely, they still have hours to go. Hours and hours that will be spent staring into a hole in the wall, waiting for something that is not going to emerge.

I use the bags for just a little while and only as required. It all depends on what I find inside, how well I can connect to it, how well it can connect me to everything else. You can tell instantly. The second I open one, I know if it is going to work or not. A good bag is a miracle, intimate and distant at the same time; completely mine and completely not mine. When everything is in order, a good bag stolen from LAX at precisely this time of year shows me a way out, a way through.

I know it may sound unorthodox, but you cannot access what I want to access without also taking some risks. And though there may be simpler, more permissible, ways to do this, again, believe me: they do not give the same results. It is possible that even you have felt it once, a little tremor of what I feel, as you wandered the aisles of the Salvation Army and contemplated the stories behind all this human merchandise. Or maybe, there was a rare occasion when you dipped your hand well below the surface of the lost and found bin, and you groped around down there, even though you knew, you knew, there was nothing in this box that could ever have belonged to you. These might be slender approximations of what I do, bare beginnings, but they are not the same. I am not searching for something that has been lost or abandoned. The bags I like most are full of essential objects, the things we need, and I love the way these possessions hold on to the energy of the original people. When I do my part and I plug in—when I snip and unzip and open and lift—I feel this power flowing through my body, and for as long as I can make it last, one evening, a weekend at most, I try to keep us both here, me and the original people, together, in the same place at the same time.

I want so badly to make you understand.

Once, for example, in a medium-sized red Samsonite, I found a travelling salesman's collection of sample toupées, dozens of them, in all the different colours and styles and lengths, each neatly packed into its own special plastic bag. When I opened the suitcase, the first flash of all that hair frightened me, as though the bag was exposing itself in some vulgar way. I slammed it closed right away, deeply ashamed, but when I peeked again, this time more curious than scared, my second thought was taxidermy. Maybe a kit, full of rare samples of hide and fur. But then, in the top pocket, I found the stack of promotional brochures, and underneath, in a separate layer, the mirrors and the metal combs and the super-adhesive gluing paper that, I suppose, has to be cut to the proper size of the bald spot so that it can fasten the hair directly to the scalp. There were instructions for how to properly measure the exposed part of the crown and temple, and how clients should change their habits to better sleep with a toupée, or bathe with a toupée, or anticipate the wind or wear a baseball cap while also wearing a toupée. The full-colour ads promised women would "want more from you" if you purchased one of these.

It was all wonderfully complicated, with so many rules and strategies. Though I am balding myself, I had never considered the possibilities. I removed each toupée, tried it on, and watched myself changing and changing each time into what seemed like a wholly new person. Once, I put on three of them at the same time—a blond side part, a curly redhead, and your basic brown—but the effect wasn't even slightly funny. When I was done, I wrote my standard note (*Sorry for the mix-up!*) and I placed it in a white envelope with five one-hundred-dollar bills. Then I returned it to the airport after just one night.

Another time, it was nothing but children's things in a brown bag with no outward markings to suggest its contents. I am not like that. Children's things are wasted on me. There were no clothes inside, just stuffed animals and toys and activities to fill the time. I imagined a long car ride. Colouring books and crayons, and a brand-new Slinky, still in the box. A Slinky, in case you do not know—I did not know—is a loose spring that is supposed to walk down the stairs by itself while it makes a slinkety sound. My hotel room, of course, had no stairs so

I tried to make it take that single decisive step off the edge of the bed, but it did not work and, in the end, I just held it in my hands as I moved the coils up and down and felt the weight sliding left to right and back again.

The other toy was a View-Master, a kind of cross between a camera and a set of binoculars that can show pictures. The shell was made of a hard red plastic and there was a slot on the top into which you inserted a white circle of thick card stock paper. The circle holds a sequence of tiny photographic nega-tives, or maybe it is the images themselves. You look through the eyeholes of the View-Master and you point it towards a light source, a window or a lamp, and every time you pull down on the trigger, or the plunger or whatever it is, the circle advances. One picture leaves and there is a second of blackness before the new one arrives. Every circle has its own theme and the child had dozens of them in a cardboard case. Stills from movies and TV shows—*The Partridge Family* and *Looney Tunes* and *The Six Million Dollar Man*—exotic animals, wide vistas, landscapes from around the world: salt fields, jungles, waterfalls, and volcanoes.

There was also a stuffed giraffe, an object so marked by its rela-tionship to another person that I almost couldn't touch it. The seams along the neck had been broken and resewn so many times that the poor thing could hardly hold up its own head anymore and instead kept flopping over in my hands. Both its glassy brown eyes were still there, sewn in place, but one of its ears and one of its nubby horns—the ones on the left side—had been sucked or chewed away. It would have taken years and years to do that, I thought, to disintegrate the fabric like that, using just human saliva, no teeth, never tearing anything away. I am familiar with this process—the sucking and the disintegrating—because, when he was very young, my little brother used to suck the middle two fingers of his right hand very hard while he slept. Eventually, he pulled those two fingernails right out of the flesh and the skin above his second knuckle stayed wet, white, and puckered all day. My parents made him wear a mitten to bed, taped around the wrist, and there were bandages for the daytime. They even coated his fingers with hot sauce, but nothing worked. Then, for no reason at all, I think the summer after he turned eight, he just grew out of it and moved on to the next thing.

The faded brown-beige splotches of this giraffe's hide were also stained with what I assumed to be old mustard and ketchup, and that raw, most basic kind of darkly familiar, impossible-to-remove dirt that sinks into everything that has spent too much time too close to one person. I slept with it for only a single late-afternoon nap and I went through all the View-Master circles two or three times, before I repackaged everything and took it back to the airport the very same day with an extra two hundred in the envelope. Seven altogether. The child—I could not tell for sure if it was a boy or a girl—would have been without their things for only a couple of hours, a minor inconvenience, I told myself.

People with no experience in what I do probably think that it always goes like this, and that every bag is full of toupées and Slinkys and giraffes. They might think this business is nothing but hidden secrets and idiosyncrasy and mystery. Perhaps they imagine that no two suitcases are alike and each one is like a fingerprint indexed to just one singular person in the world. *The things you've seen*, they might think, if they ever thought of me. Every suitcase jammed to the edges, straining at its zipper, ready to burst with the intensity of a disclosure.

It would be wonderful if this were true. And maybe, at least in the beginning, I yearned for it. Maybe this was the thing I was looking for. Some proof of our infinity, each person carrying around their own small signature portion of the limitless difference that makes us all exactly who we are.

Unfortunately, the truth is another story. I have pored through the evidence and the results I have found are not encouraging. Judged by our suitcases—at least the hundreds I have personally inspected—I am sorry to inform you that there is almost nothing of interest happening in this world and we are mostly interchangeable. Like an archaeologist sifting through our dig site a thousand years in the future, I have come down through all the layers and swept away everything else and held the essential uncovered artifacts in my hands. This is why I feel so well positioned to tell you, objectively, that for most of us, our main concerns barely extend beyond our underwear and the things we need for the bathroom.

I am, of course, ashamed and embarrassed by all of this. As I should be. But I am ashamed not just for myself, not just because of the things I do, but for all of us. Most likely, I would be ashamed of you too, embarrassed by the things you carry so close to yourself, the way you pack. I can't tell you how bad it gets sometimes, the way, in just seconds, the potential high can crash to a dangerous low. If I open one more suitcase and I find one more of those pale, blue-collared shirts folded into a perfect square with its sleeves tucked behind its back and its chest puffed out, I don't know what I will do. Though I am not a violent person, the last time that happened I drew my fist back all the way and I punched that shirt straight through its smug little line of buttons. Same for all the sundresses and the floppy hats and the jewellery and the ridiculous footwear selections, two or three pairs of sandals for the same trip. The bathing suits often still have the price tags attached! Can you imagine how disappointing that is? To go through everything I have gone through: to take the risks, to invest your money and your time and your hope, to bring your pliers—or to purchase the emergency bolt cutters if they are needed—and yet, in the end, to find yourself nowhere, just back at the same local shopping mall, standing again beside another spinning sale rack.

The toiletries are always disgusting. People do things to themselves that I cannot understand. Tweezers and Q-tips and razors and cotton balls. Little brushes and lotions and creams that are supposed to either protect you or open you up to the sun. There is dental floss or there isn't, deodorant or not. Travel-sized versions of plug-in appliances that will dry or straighten or curl your hair. None of these choices seem to matter. I feel no aversion to using another person's toothbrush, so I usually do that, at the very least. And then, of course, I wait until the bristles are completely dry (sometimes I even use the hair dryer for this job) before I put it back again exactly, exactly as I found it.

I think this is okay. I think it is even good for the original people to have to wonder about this, to ask themselves this one basic question when they get the bag back. Was there or was there not contact? It is the most basic question, but when you get the standard bag—the bag that is our shared nothing—what other option is there? I consider the toothbrush to be a bare minimum. But it is so, so boring, let me tell you, to go through the whole ritual and then to just stand there, looking at yourself in the mirror, with the bristles in your mouth and a plastic handle in your hand. A person runs through everything else, a person goes right to the limit, but if there is nothing to work with, there is nothing to work with. What could possibly be gained from trying on a dry-cleaned skirt still wrapped in the flimsiest cellophane?

Before this happened, before Tanya's bag sent me off course, I believed the thing I really wanted, the thing I had been hoping to find though it had eluded me for years, was the bag of someone coming home, a suitcase that belonged to a person just finishing their journey after a long time away. A local, somebody actually from Los Angeles. I could imagine them sleeping through their alarm in Minnesota, then rushing around and throwing the jumble together as fast as they could—sweaters and dirty socks, maybe a book. Some things would be forgotten and others accidentally stolen. Or I pictured a relationship, two people under the gun, rushing against a schedule, but so intimately connected to each other that their things, maybe a man's and a woman's things, could be tossed into the same bag to be sorted out later. I would love to find that, a single suitcase with two lives already mixed up in it, completely its own, completely itself, and then completely mine for a little while. I would like to feel a part of that, to join in in my way, to smell their bodies still sitting there inside their clothes, not faded away yet. I would like to feel that, but so far, it has not happened.

Tanya's bag, though, is not like that. It is extraordinary. I opened it two days ago and I have been searching through it ever since. You see it in pirate movies sometimes, or after the big heist of the crown jewels, or the successful bank robbery: they open an old wooden chest or a stainless-steel briefcase and all the criminals gather around because what is inside—the ruby-encrusted goblets or the pile of raw diamonds sitting on a bed of black velvet—is actually radiating, throbbing with yellow energy. That is what it was like when the light from the hotel room bulb hit the sequins in Tanya's uniform at precisely the spot where the cream white bodice meets the purple stripe that goes across the chest. I did not know exactly what it was at first. I had never seen or even imagined something like this existing in the world, never given it any of my own thoughts, though now, obviously, I understand there are people, whole massively coordinated teams of people, who think of little else.

I looped my index fingers into the shoulder straps and I lifted it out of the bag. It was a one-piece—and I guess it is shaped like a bathing suit, but much more substantial. Very, very heavy, specially tailored, and structured on the inside with a kind of ribbing that must support the breasts and keep everything secure in a certain way. It is a real uniform, professionally made, unforgiving and extremely tight, and entirely covered in these white and purple sequins they must have to sew on individually, maybe even by hand. The person inside would not be allowed to be overweight. Most likely she would have to change her body to fit her clothes and not the other way around. Her name was written in purple marker on the tag.

Everything else was there too, all the different required elements in their own separate smaller bags. Two pairs of beige tights, thick and heavy, and the long, perfectly polished white knee-high boots with their elevated heels. White gloves that went way past the elbow and a tackle box of theatrical makeup and glitter. Also, multiple sets of false eyelashes with more glue-on adhesive. A plastic tiara and a tin full of bobby pins. Even the baton itself, its two halves ready to be screwed together and the two clear weighted bobbles. These four parts were all in a green plastic box branded *Twirl World*, with the name of the squad stencilled below it: *The Assumption Purple Raiders*. They would have had to pay extra for that. If I owned the company, I would make them pay extra for personalization.

I felt sure that something like this, the ensemble a majorette has to wear, would not come cheap, even if it was part of the team set, a full order the school had made from some company in the Midwest that specializes in this kind of thing. I thought of the bake sales and the car washes and the fundraising drives. A trip for all of them to Southern California. It would be a once-in-a-lifetime experience. I imagined the rehearsals every night after school and on the weekends. Competing against the other squads, winning the regional championship, and earning their right to be here. Just getting to this stage, qualifying, it would mean everything to them, everything to her. I felt the urgency, the excitement and the loss, and, for the first time in my life, I saw my part in all of it, the problem and the possibility.

—

I do not follow sports so I am only slightly embarrassed to admit that, before this happened, I had never heard of the "Rose Bowl" or its famous parade. And though I am actually in the middle of it now, I guess, here in the staging area at seven in the morning, surrounded by the music and the dancers and the hundred thousand glued flowers, I must tell you, again, that none of this rich pageantry, not one part of this spectacle enacted on such a grand scale, is remotely interesting to me. I am trying the hardest I have ever tried, and yet I still cannot see what the others see. All this excess for what? Sometimes, I think people carry things too far.

On my way here, for example, searching for Tanya's group, I must have passed more than a dozen of these massive flatbed float contraptions. One had a gigantic animatronic bird that was at least fifty feet tall. The door of his chest was open as I walked by, and I watched the technicians warming him up, studying the hydraulics inside the machine. During the parade, I guess this bird will dip its head again and again, and every time he will pull out the same twenty-foot worm. The worm is bluish-green and, believe it or not, he is smiling and holding a sign that says *Spring is almost here!*

Then I came upon an underwater kingdom—mermaids and shells and huge styrofoam sea horses—then a dog catcher van driven by dogs, with uniformed people in the cage behind. Then Tarzan swinging on his vines. Swans and superheroes, and a pair of tethered, three-storey-high balloons—Sylvester the Cat and Tweety Bird. There were two teams of a dozen teenagers each charged with hauling these things down the road, trying not to get pulled off the ground by any sudden gusts. It stretched on and on like that in the staging area, one absurdity after the other, piled on top of each other before they began their journey down the route. I passed nine other marching bands, and one other set of "Raiders," before I found my purple ones.

I come from a colder place. And, normally, those are the conditions in which I feel most comfortable. I don't think the Californians could ever understand. Maybe they imagine the winter as a period of brutal isolation, but those of us who live in the snow, those of us who appreciate the turn of the seasons and look forward to the shift from summer to fall, we know otherwise. Cold is a better companion than heat; it makes room for you. A person can negotiate with cold, work out a better relationship, add more to the mix if you need to, pull on another layer. That is why I always wear these gloves when I am here, thin gloves even in the heat. I like to work that extra membrane. I like to have more of a say about the way I touch things and the way things touch me.

But that is not how it works in the hotter places. There are limits to how much you can subtract, how much you can take away or take off. And once a person is completely naked under the sun, there is no more room to negotiate. I see the girls in the parks here, lying on their bellies, directly on the grass, without even a sheet or a towel beneath them, their skin touched by thousands of individual blades. They read their books and they drink their Cokes and they listen to their radios. Sometimes they just lie there with their eyes closed. During these moments, they wear only their bathing suit bottoms and the clasps that normally hold their tops together are unhooked and flayed out on both sides so that their backs, the Vs of their shoulder blades, and the parallel lines of their ribs are fully exposed. I feel for them, but I do not know exactly what it is that I feel. Mostly, I think I want to bring them a blanket. I want them somehow to feel warmer, though here, outside in the air, it is ninety degrees. Warmer, not hotter. You understand the difference.

Clothes are fuller when there are people inside them pushing to get out. I notice this as I watch Tanya's team move through their stretching routine. I have run my fingers over every sequin of this outfit and I have embraced it, crushing the fabric against my chest to feel the ribbing and its deep internal structure. I even slept beside it last night, me under the covers on my side, the left, and the whole costume above the blankets on the right, the boots and the gloves and the tiara and the baton, perfectly arranged and flat on their back, facing the ceiling. Now, though, as I see the full ensemble repeating and repeating in front of me, crouching and spinning, even extending its legs into the air, the design seems to have taken on a new, almost random, life of its own.

I admire the discipline of these women, the crisp precision of their actions. Though we are still in the staging area—a park and a parking lot, and blocks of closed-off city streets—and it is still early in the morning, the entire performance is going on right here. They stand in formation, each one at the centre of her own living sphere, and, in perfect synchronicity, they hurl their batons into the air. Then they count together while they turn in quick circles with their arms outstretched. Someone on the sideline claps out a beat—"Three, and four, and five!"— and then, right on the five, they all kick their left legs high above their heads and they extend their arms, palms flat and reaching, and somehow the batons return on time, dropping out of the sky and landing where they want, precisely when they need them to be there. The legs snap down and the twirling begins, the weighted rod flowing from hand to hand and even around their necks. It seems like this cycle—the throw, the spin, the kick, the catch, and the twirl—can run on, over and over again, almost forever. Around them, the drums beat and the clarinets blare, the arms of trombonists reach all the way out before they come back in, but the focus of the major-ettes remains intense and absolute. They are not distracted, as I am, by the epauletted trumpet players or the swaying fringe or the barking of their leaders.

When I first found them, my particular group of Raiders, I approached cautiously. Behind my glasses, I scanned for her—the gap in their formation, a girl missing the thing she needed most. I imagined her standing off to the side, disappointed, and not yet aware that I am here now, and I will change things for the better. But I could not find her anywhere.

With so much going on, there was plenty of cover, so I waited for my opportunity. When I thought everyone was look-ing the other way, I placed the bag beside that tree, over by the rest of their gear. Close enough to belong, far enough to be sep-arate. I wanted her to notice it even if she couldn't understand it: the impossible return. Then I retreated to this position, fifty feet away, and I began my vigil.

This was thirteen minutes ago, but nothing has happened yet, and I fear perhaps it is already too late. I have carried this bag for miles, walking entirely under my own power, something I never do. And I came this way only because I wanted to be here in person to witness it—the reunion, and the relief washing over her. It will be my first time, my first experience being this close, and I know that everything is in order, perfectly repacked and ready to go. And we should still have plenty of time. The parade does not begin for at least another hour and she could change and be ready in five minutes. Somebody just needs to see. Somebody needs to understand the significance of what is right in front of them.

Maybe just one more nudge to push it over the edge.

I make my decision, my weight shifts, and I am about to step forward and call her name when I feel a hand on my shoulder. It clamps down hard.

I turn and it is an older woman, in her sixties probably, but she is wearing a purple Raiders jacket. Her eyes are clear and she has the posture of a person who used to be an athlete, shoulders back and square.

"What exactly do you think you're looking at?" she asks me.

Maybe in the end, all we want is a little bit of perspective. And that is what they give you here, in California, early in the morning, on the first day of January. I know there is winter light in the middle of the desert, or on top of a mountain, or even filtered down to the floor of the rainforest. But it is not like this, not light with all of us inside of it at the same time. Not light coming straight down on a city of millions.

Normally, I try to keep track of the shadows and watch how they retreat back to us throughout the morning before extending away again in the evening. I wait for that instant, at noon, when everything becomes just itself. The dogs and the trees, the fire hydrants, benches, and telephone booths. The skyscrapers and doughnut shops. This woman in front of me, that boy over there resting against his tuba. For one moment, when the light is directly overhead, it feels like all the darkness is burned away and nothing is blurred at the edges anymore. A person comes to this place to be a solid object, a thing in the world alongside all the other things. That, at least, is why I come, so that I can be close to them though I am not one of them.

"Pardon me?" I say.

In the middle of the formation, one of the majorettes stops her practising. She steps out of the group and comes forward, her face changing, sharpening. Our eyes lock and she points the end of her baton, her crystal ball, directly at the middle of my chest.

"That one," she says. "Him."

The coach looks at her and then back at me. Her hand is still on my shoulder. The majorette moves her baton from my chest down my body, then over, along the sidewalk, to the bag resting by the tree.

"He dumped that bag," the majorette says. "It's one of ours, a backup from last year's team. We packed three of those blue ones, just in case something got lost."

I turn and shake free of the woman's clamped hand and start to walk away.

"Sorry about the mix-up," I call out over my shoulder. And then I start to jog, then run, then sprint towards the anonymous crowd of thousands that waits just around the corner. I know that all I have to do is get there and it will be okay.

"Stop!" the coach yells. "That man, stop him."

I often think about consequences. Sometimes, I even dream about them. An ordering power that will finally put me in my place. Like this woman and the entire marching band she commands. I imagine her sending them to chase after me, the purple feathers in their hats bobbing up and down. I can picture it: getting caught at last, my body completely encircled and me standing in the middle, a boy threatening to beat me with a xylophone. But it does not go that way.

Instead, they give up almost immediately and I escape, utterly untouched, again. This is because they have more important things to do today, and I do not really matter in the grand scheme.

Still, though, I do wonder about my Tanya.

Is she even here, in Southern California, at the Rose Bowl Parade, right now? Is she still part of the team? Does she remain an Assumption Purple Raider? Or is it possible that all of this— the bag and the band, the costumes, the coaches, the practising, and the whole routine—is already in her past? I would like to meet her if I could and ask my questions and explain myself. I think I could do it. I think I could make her understand what happened when I held her uniform in my hands. Her fitted suit, her tights and her boots and her gloves, her tiara, her bobby pins and her eyelashes. I would like Tanya to know that I kept these things safe, and I did my best to bring them all back to her. I want her to know that I took special care and, if she wants, if she is free, perhaps we could meet when the show is over and all the confusion has been sorted out. We could do whatever she likes, fly wherever she wishes to go, because there is no cost in this world that is too great for me bear. I can pay, and I will pay, for everything.

EVERYTHING UNDERNEATH

THIS IS ABOUT ME AND MY SISTER. OR IS IT MY SISTER and *I*, or my sister and *me*?

It is 1982 and we are at the beach, not doing anything, really. Just trying to hold our spots and take up as much space as we can while we float face down in water that is slightly above our heads, maybe seven feet deep. Arms and legs wide, splayed out and sunburnt, we stare through plastic and make gasping sounds when we breathe. *Ta* and *ta* and *ta*. Water mixed with spit mixed with air, sloshing in our matching orange tubes. Our mom picked up both masks and both snorkels at an end-of-the-season two-for-one blowout and we wanted to try them right away.

It is bright and everything underneath pulses like it is extra alive. The mask is brand new, still clean and super transparent, almost as if there could be something clearer than perfectly clear. It sharpens the edges of every separate thing, and you can even see individual grains of sand moving in the current, and watch the waves running backwards. Or, I guess, I feel that more than I see it, the flow going around my body, the way the whole world down here is always moving, and it all has to go back out the same way it came in. The exact same water, and the exact same amount of it, just quieter and less frothy when it's rolling below in the opposite direction.

We are not very good. And though we try to scull our hands and kick at the perfect pace to stay in position, I still feel the tug, like there is a loose rope wound around our ankles, getting ready to draw us out to the real bottomless part of the ocean.

A girl in my class, Melinda, did a project on this once. We could choose any energy source we wanted—wind or solar or whatever, any of the alternatives—but she decided to go with *TIDAL POWER!* I remember how the words were cut out in alternating blue and green letters and glued to the top of the same three-fold bristol board display we all had to use for our projects. She was a good drawer, and I can still see it perfectly: so neat and well-organized and easy to understand.

For the middle panel, she had a diagram of an underwater turbine resting on the bottom of the Bay of Fundy, and she had a cool way of using dots and arrows to show how the water figure-eighted as it came in from one side, then looped around a few hours later to go back through the other way. It was like one of those *Family Circus* cartoons with all the intersecting footprints. During her seven-minute presentation, she read from index cards and gestured stiffly at one thing and then the next. She told us that all of this was because of the moon and outer space.

That's what this girl was saying.

I was sitting at my desk, mostly thinking about my own presentation, and running over what I was going to tell them about the pros and cons of my nuclear reactor, but when she got to that part, I had to look up. Melinda was waving her arm around, above the display, above our heads, and she was telling us that the moon was pushing around all the water in the world.

She kept it coming with the facts, one card after another. All the awesome clean megawattage we'd be able to harness if we could just find a way. Because the moon was reliable, she explained, and all this water had places it had to get to on time, and there were experts who knew exactly when it was going to be where it was going to be. There was nothing new about this part, she said. People who paid attention to the sea had always known. Like fishermen. For them, the ocean was more predictable than maybe we thought.

She got to her last card. "In conclusion," she said, but I was already done, and I thought it then, just like I think it now.

You're telling me the *moon* is doing *this*?

Unlikely, Melinda. *Very* unlikely.

——

It isn't a private beach or anything, not a secret place. Just the shore beside a family-owned campground. But we have been coming here once or twice a summer all our lives. Our mom likes it. The cliffs cut down very steeply on both sides, so it feels almost like another world, and there is a warm, shallow brook that winds across the sand before feeding out. When we were smaller, we used to spend all our time in there, in the fresh water, just up to our knees, or a little bit off to the side with our plastic buckets and shovels, building sandcastles and moats and dams out of driftwood. Sometimes, we would bury each other. One of us would have to lie on her back while the other one scooped and shovelled and scooped a million times until the person underneath was just a face sticking out and the sand pushed down super heavy on her chest.

We used to not be allowed to go into the big ocean at all.

"I want you always here and never there, okay?" our mom would say. And she'd point one finger at the brook and the other at the waves.

This was a couple of summers ago. We didn't have the masks yet, and we couldn't really swim—we can barely swim now—so we never had the chance to see what this place looks like. It's just different when you're completely inside the water or staring down from above.

I guess it's like a movie—maybe everything is like a movie—but this isn't us just *watching* a movie. This feels like we are *making* the movie, a real nature documentary, and we get to shoot it all by ourselves, focusing on all the right details at the right time. Then we call in the British guy at the end to do the voice-over.

"The striped bass," he will say. "The lobster. Behold!"

And they are both right there. The lobster, so brown he's black, just walking over the rocks below with his claws up in the air. Or not up in the air, obviously. You know what I mean. The lobster is walking around with his claws up in the water. And then our bored fish, a striped bass, just hanging out. He opens his mouth and he closes it. His gills flap.

The sun on my back feels like it is tilting towards too hot, and I wonder how long we've been here like this. Just watching and watching. It isn't anything, really: only sand and rocks, and a twist of human metal, I think a bedframe or an old-fashioned box spring that has been down here for years. Then one lazy bass and a strolling lobster. It's not like we're talking about Hawaii and it's not like this is a coral reef, full of wild colours and impossible animals you can barely believe. All we have is Nova Scotia and whatever is in the water close to the shore.

But it still feels so super old. That's the other thing I can't stop thinking about. It's like all of this, the little events that are happening down here, all the stuff we're looking at for the first time, has been happening and happening and happening, in this same spot, in the same way, almost since the beginning of the whole world.

My sister reaches down and picks up a hermit crab, its shell about the size of a piece of popcorn. She pinches it between her finger and her thumb and lifts. As soon as she touches it, as soon as her skin even grazes its shell, the crab pulls all the way back and pretends to be a rock, a nothing pebble in her palm, waiting her out. Then when she drops it again, boom, it's back on and scurrying fast, trying to find some cover or crawl under anything big enough to get away from her, get away from us, whatever it thinks we are.

The mouthpiece still has a chemical factory taste, but you have to lick it and squeeze the black rubber pegs as gently as you can, with just your cheeks and your lips. Can't bite too hard or clench with your jaw. Just hold it there. And you have to keep breathing. You have to calm down. You have to concentrate. There is a secret to it, a technique that other people have mastered. You want to suck the air out of the sky and blow it back through this little narrow space. That's the exchange, slow and steady.

Ta and *ta* and *ta*. We find our rhythm and it gets easier. I give my sister the thumbs-up sign like a real scuba diver, and she nods. I think she even smiles, her top lip squishing up against the clear nosepiece. It feels almost like a real connection. Normally, on land, we can't stand each other. It takes her forever to get ready for anything, and even as we were running here, into the waves, I didn't like how she moved her legs. She always seems slanted to me, especially when she's trying to go quickly. It's like she's all tipped over and bent too far to one side.

Me and my sister. My sister and I. My sister and me. It has never been good between us. Never. We are eleven months apart and we have the same parents—the same mom, right there, on a blanket at the beach, reading her book, and the same dad, wherever he is now. But we have always had this gap, too. Eleven months is too close, and at the same time, it is too far away.

—

Earlier this summer, we had some drama with a trampoline and we are not over it yet. It wasn't our trampoline. Just a trampoline. It is 1982, remember, and before we saw it, we imagined no normal individual could possibly possess a trampoline of their own. You would need to be in the circus, or training for the Olympics or something. But there it was: unexpected and unbounced-upon, sitting in the middle of an overgrown yard, behind an unknown house we'd never been to before.

The lady we were visiting was someone our mom used to know. A person she was trying to reach back to.

"Gina," she kept insisting on the drive there. "Gina, for God's sake. You remember Gina. We talk about her all the time. Me and Gina. Gina and me. We were such good friends. It hasn't been *that* long since the last time. Come on. You have been there. I'm telling you that you *have* been here. You just don't remember."

There were no kids living at the house with the trampoline. Or no kids anymore, or at least no evidence of their presence. Just a black rectangle taking up a third of the yard, a scorching sheet of nylon with grass growing up through its springs and all around. The way the green and the black came together, one surrounding the other, made it look like a massive hole, or a work zone, maybe, a huge excavation pit in the middle of the yard.

Gina saw us staring at it through the back window.

"That thing," she said, and she shook her head. "Don't know what I'm going to do with it now. Impossible to take apart."

She had already laid out the plate of store-bought cookies, and a room-temperature two-litre bottle of cola, and a stainless-steel bowl of the cheapest kind of cheezies you can buy, the ones with too much air blown into them.

She and Mom had wine and real Triscuits and Ritzes and Vegetable Thins and two kinds of fancy cheese on a wooden chopping board.

We looked at their stuff, and our stuff, then back outside.

That was a trampoline out there.

"Go ahead," Gina said, and she waved us through the sliding doors. "Knock yourself out."

Then she circled her hand over the snacks like she was casting a spell. To me, at that moment, the cheezies seemed extra orange and extra dry and extra hollow.

"Don't worry," she said. "This will all be here when you come back."

Then the women clinked their glasses and laughed.

"At last," I heard my mom say as we left the room. "I can't wait for you to tell me all about it."

As we slid open the patio doors, my sister cut me off and elbowed me in the stomach and turned her shoulders sideways so she could slip through the crack ahead of me. I watched her do her tilted sprinting across the lawn and how she kicked off her shoes in the last two steps and then flung herself over the metal edge to climb up onto the bouncing part.

We are not the same size, me and my sister. And we do not have the same build. And we never will. I think we both understand this already. A person gets to know another person's body. Especially if that body is around you all the freaking time, and you have to share your bedroom with it, and even sleep in the same bed with it, under the same covers, for several years. Every night and every morning, the other body is right there. And the two of you, you and this body, you end up getting too comfortable or maybe too uncomfortable. The other person keeps changing in front of you, ripping all their stuff off, right down to nothing, and leaving their super-gross underwear in the middle of the floor.

It's just that we're different people, my sister and I, and it's impossible not to notice. I think about it a lot. Her hair and my hair, the way some of it is curly and some of it is flat. Or my skin and her skin, the way it reacts under the sun. Or our legs and arms, my middle and her middle, lengths and thicknesses. Something in our coding must be off, and somewhere deep inside our bodies, inside the inside of our cells, I know there are key sequences that we do not share. No one way of sneezing, no common set of eyebrows, no two pairs of double-jointed thumbs. Nothing uncannily similar. We could never be mistaken for sisters.

It's probably nothing, but I wonder sometimes about all the ways we are not the same. And I wonder if there is something wrong with us, or if it might be better if the situation were different. Different from the different we already have. And I wonder if this will ever count, or even be noticed, by anybody else. Like sometimes, I imagine us when we are more grown up and other people start coming around and maybe they want to kiss us or do whatever. People we don't know yet. Really good-looking people we haven't met, but maybe they will want to be with us someday.

Maybe one of them will have a preference, a certain type of body they like more than another type of body. I think about that a lot, a lot: the super-good-looking people in my future. And I want to do better in that department. Whenever these people finally show up, I want them to like me way more than they like her.

Maybe school is right. All the stuff they tell us in health class, and all the dumb pamphlets they hand out. Maybe this is just an intense stage we're in right now and this phase will eventually pass, but I feel like I can see everything all at once and I'm always comparing. This girl or guy over that girl or guy. And these shows and those songs. And our teachers: the ones who are trying too hard to be cool and the ones who stink and always wear the same outfits every Tuesday and Thursday. And all the parents and the amounts of money they make. All the obvious ways it shows. A real polo shirt with a real polo guy holding up a real polo mallet, or the other one, the fake, just a purple guy with no stick at all, riding on a purple horse. Madonna over Cyndi Lauper, but Belinda Carlisle more beautiful than both. Nobody wants to admit it, but someone is always doing better than someone else.

On a trampoline, though, that pressure kind of disappears, at least for a second. A trampoline with no net or enclosure, with nothing surrounding it, just the open sky. You get to throw yourself around for a little while, and it feels like you're in, then temporarily out, of your body. My sister and me, it took us a couple of passes, but we eventually hit on the pattern that every two people on a trampoline eventually figure out. When one is up, the other is down, but it's not a big deal. It's actually fine. That's how it has to go. One boing, followed by the next. And one switcheroo and then another and another.

The black sheet of the bouncing surface was way firmer than we expected. Maybe because of the old springs, tighter and rustier. And we went much, much higher than I thought we would.

In the beginning, I tried to focus only on my sister's hair. And I watched for the little delay, the way the separate strands landed on her shoulders just as she was about to go up again, and then, at the apex, how they spread out in a big circle around her head, like one of those halos from the science centre demonstration, even though the rest of her was already descending. There is this moment, a split second on either end of the up and the down, when you don't know if you're finished yet, and you're not sure if this is the top of the top or the bottom of the bottom.

I can't explain why it happened. We'd passed each other dozens of times already, freeze-framing into all the regular poses, the easy tricks everyone tries when they are just starting out. Knees curled to the chest. Then the opposite, the spread-eagled, toe-touching splits. A couple of plunging sits, where you bounce back to standing after ricocheting off your butt. And my sister even attempted one or two tentative somersaults, pulling her chin down fast and swinging her arms hard and backwards to start the front flip. I still don't know how to do that.

And I still don't know why she stopped without telling me, without any signal, like I wasn't even there. My sister. She just decided that she had had enough, and this was a good time to take a rest. One second she was going up and it was all good, but then, as she came down, she bent her knees very, very deep, almost to a full squat. And this absorbed almost all the bounce so that she would not go back up.

You understand that this changed everything for me. While I was in the air, our momentum flipped around, and the coordinated wave we'd been boinging back and forth through the black sheet turned the wrong way. I didn't sense it then, I couldn't see it coming, but I have it figured out now, and in my mind I can slow the scene down till it's flipping just one frame at a time. As I was descending, the trampoline was going up, rebounding off my sister. And instead of absorbing me, it resisted, pushing back with no give at all. Instead of a sheet, it was a rising floor.

The tip of my tongue got caught between my teeth and when the down and the up collided, I snipped it clean through.

I hope this never happens to you. There are like a billion million nerve endings in the tip of the tongue and all of mine went off at the same time.

Before it all turned bad, there was this flash and we both saw it. This sliver of my tongue, completely separate from me, but still moving against the black like a worm on a leaf.

The thing I felt next was maybe the purest kind of hurt combined with the purest kind of anger. It just erupted out of me.

"I hate you so much!" I screamed.

My tongue was already swelling, and the red was spilling out of my mouth. In five more seconds, it would be as big as a closed fist and I wouldn't be able to talk at all. But I got it out.

"You did that on purpose. I wish you were dead!"

She looked at me—I can't tell you what that look was like, I couldn't process it right—but she shook her head, and then she kneeled down and, so gently, she picked up the piece of my tongue and cradled it in her palm.

"Oh my God," she said. And then, "Come on. Come with me. We have to go."

She reached out to me and put her hand under my armpit and helped me over the edge.

No cookies, no cola, no cheezies.

Instead, Kleenex, and paper towels, and ice cubes wrapped in a wet red-and-white-checkered dishtowel.

Mom and Gina drained their glasses and I remember the way Mom billowed her cheeks out like a trumpet player. She looked at Gina.

"It never ends," she said.

"Nope," Gina replied. "Never ever, ever."

But then she smiled and waved at us as we pulled out of her driveway.

"Thank you, Dee," she said. "At least for the first part. We'll have to try again. Sooner next time, okay?"

Then the three of us driving erratically to the hospital, me with the numbing dishtowel squished up against my face and everyone else silent. And then the three of us sitting for six hours in the emergency room. And then nothing helpful.

"Just keep the ice on there and wait it out," the doctor said. "You'll see. Wet tissue heals fast. Maybe gargle with salt water? Not much else we can do. Should be back to normal in a couple of days."

"What about this?" my sister asked. And she showed her the piece of tongue, resting on an ice cube in a styrofoam coffee cup. I hadn't realized she'd been holding it all day and refreshing the ice cubes. My flesh was grey now.

"Sorry," the doctor said. "Give that to me and I'll make sure it gets disposed of properly."

"So we're not going to sew it back on?"

"No," she said, "we are not."

—

This reminds me of that. The basic taste of salt inside of water. At home, I had to gargle every three hours, and even after I stirred in the spoonful, sometimes the grit would stay in the glass and I could still feel the solid crystals swirling inside my cheeks before I spit it back out.

Out here, it's like that, but somehow the taste is stronger even though there's nothing solid left. So weird when you think about all the salt that's been totally absorbed into the ocean, whole mountain ranges of it, suspended in the water.

This day—a picnic and one last trip to the beach—was supposed to be the end of it for us, the closing down of summer. One last free afternoon before the locking in of another year and the return to school and work and routine. Warm and easy, that was the original plan. Naps and bodysurfing and drinks from the cooler, listening to the radio, walks on the sand. We never saw this coming. This level of activity. The snorkels and the masks were just sitting there in a discounted wire bin, beside all the leftover camping gear and the squirt guns and bug spray, and the price was too good to let them go.

Each set came in its own mesh bag with a drawstring and a spring-loaded toggle, but we decided not to use the flippers today. For maybe two minutes we tried, stomping around our towels, but the tight plastic place where you're supposed to wedge your foot felt too hard and too dry and it pulled out the hairs I didn't even know I had down there. I think, now, that maybe you're supposed to carry the fins to the water first, and then you soak the foot part before slipping them on when you're already inside. Next time, we will know better, but you understand what it's like. We were too excited, and it felt like too much unnecessary hassle. The footprints we left behind looked like they came from a giant prehistoric bird that had been sniffing around our stuff.

I watch my sister in the water again and I study the way she works her fingers. Spread wide, with as much space as she can possibly get between her separate digits. She wants everything to flow through.

Then I look down at my own hands. Cupped tight into almost solid paddles so that I can push against the water and move myself around.

You see it, and you see it, every single day—the things your sister does that are not the things that you do—and every single day, you have the same questions.

Why are you like that? What the hell were you thinking?

We drift apart, maybe fifteen feet. Absorbed in our own scenes now, the separate realities we need to concentrate on.

The bass notices before we do. This fish, it goes from right here to right gone. I know it must have moved—it has definitely moved—but the vanishing happened before I could register any action.

And then something else. A new presence enters the picture, and I think it is not at all like a striped bass. It slides in from the periphery. Slow and lazy and smooth, right between my sister and me, as though it has nothing to do, no purpose at all in this world. I have never seen one before in real life, but right away I feel like I know it intimately. I feel like this thing in the water has always been inside of me, or at least it has always been here with us, always distantly connected, though it normally lives so far away.

The British voice-over guy comes back to me, and it seems like he has been talking to us about this for every Sunday afternoon of our lives. All his disjointed facts so calmly narrated, so easy to say when you are only looking at a picture. Oldest animal on the planet, unchanged since the time of the dinosaurs. They never sleep, never stop moving, can't go backwards. Skeleton built entirely out of cartilage. The rolling rows of teeth, end-lessly coming forward and replacing themselves, like the spirals in a vending machine.

I look at it and my stomach clenches and I can feel the acid pouring into my centre.

Sideways and sideways and sideways, it moves. Eight, maybe nine feet long, a swaying tube of muscle. It makes a circle around us, then passes through the middle again. My eye meets its eye, perfectly round and unblinking. There is no contact, only an echo of its movement, the water pushing up against me with more force. He has a healed scar, a bubbled line maybe three feet long, running in a continuous zigzag down the side. Something from long before.

I turn to my sister and watch a flex of panic move across her face.

I can hear it in her tube too. A catch and a bad swallow. The wrong mix of air and water.

I want to send a thought across to her, a telepathic wave: *Don't move. Don't. Move. Stay right there.*

I think it through the water.

Please. Please, Becca.

Please hear what I am not saying.

They can't see well. I remember that part, too.

Like bats, kind of. So they hunt with this weird electrical sensor—I think maybe in their noses—and this thing can pick up the shock of any sudden twitch, the firing of a muscle.

It goes around us again. The blue dorsal fin, exactly like you'd picture it, and the white underbelly, and the slits on the sides, like industrial vents. Every part of it is real, and in the world, and here. Here right now with us. The long snout, the way the top and bottom jaw come together. Almost a smirk.

It has a notch in its tail and as it swings out to make a sharp turn, this rakes my sister's leg hard.

I see her wince and then, a second later, a symmetrical red pattern blooms on her thigh, like rubbing up too hard against a cheese grater.

I don't know what I am supposed to do, but I know this is bad. Even a hint of it in the water will be enough.

And at the same time, I can't stop thinking about everything else. Like the fact that this is objectively not fair. And not right. He is not supposed to be here. Not this far north. Impossible. *You belong to Australia*, I think. Or someplace like that. The shores of Tasmania. And you should never have been able to make it to Nova Scotia. Something basic, a fundamental force, should have turned you around long ago.

I send my sister a different message now. And for the first time I feel something different too. Something shifting between us. Maybe the opposite of my trampoline hate, though it probably still isn't love.

Come on, I think, and I gesture with my finger towards the shore. *Come with me. We have to go now. Nice and slow.*

The thick rubber band digs into my head too tight. Half an hour ago, I suspected that I was putting the metal peg into the wrong hole. Now I know I was right.

It turns in an erratic swishing circle, like something lost, and moves away.

I reach out for her and we turn together and make our way towards the shore.

Our mom starts yelling and I wish she would please be quiet. Please. And I wish I could see this scene, all of it at once, but from a better angle. I wish I could get there, somewhere above the water, above the sand, above Mom's head, but below the sky. A good stepladder might be enough. I just want to get out of my own head. I want to be able to look down and see only what is there.

A woman calling, and two girls, and a fin cutting the air.

"Becca?" the woman says. She is up now, running towards the shoreline. "Kate!"

Her voice wavering, but trying to hold steady. She gave them those names.

"Come back here, girls. Right now, okay? Back here. Now, please."

I touch my sister's shoulder and our eyes lock again. We are both crying inside our masks.

You and me, I think. *Me and you. You and I. What is this?* And *I'm sorry.* And *I'm such an idiot.*

I know the next five seconds will be the key. We just need to get through. The next five seconds, then the next, and the next.

Our feet find the bottom and we push forward. Sand between our toes now and sand under our fingernails as we claw our way out. We spit out the tubes and reach back behind our heads to pull at the elastics and fling the masks away. The two of us now, together and in the clear. We suck the air straight from the source, full and deep, as much as we want. Again and again.

I touch her leg and spread my fingers wide over the pattern of her wound. Water and salt mixed in, diluting her blood. It looks like there is more than there is. A breeze blowing over our heads, but I can't feel the temperature. Our mom shouting, but I can't hear her voice. The uncaring clouds. We half crawl, half slither out of the ocean and onto the shore. Like we are the first creatures to ever come this way.

THE ENTERTAINER

SCOTT JOPLIN

DARCY

The problem with this song is that everyone thinks they already know how it's supposed to go.

I haven't even started yet, but I can tell you what's going to happen during the performance and how it will end. The first three bars will be no problem. It even says you should play them "not fast," so I will roll through nice and even, right to left, down and down and down, before I drop straight into the signature theme. Then the moment of recognition will arrive, and all the people here will make the connection at the same time: *Oh yeah*, they'll think, *this is "The Entertainer."* And they'll all have the same expectations for what's coming next, especially the middle sections where you need to be so quick and clear and precise. Those are the parts they'll be looking forward to, the famous turns and switchbacks, but, even in practice, I've never come through those sections clean, and unless some miracle occurs, that is not going to change today. Right now, I am the only one who understands how bad the situation is, but in about ten minutes, my disaster is going to swallow everyone in this room.

Our little music school normally does three of these recitals every year. One for Christmas, one for "Spring," and then this one, Halloween. There's no formal evaluation, so they're more like mini concerts, about an hour long, held in the lower level of the Brookfield Retirement Living Complex. They set us up in their "social recreation" area, beside the little bar and the pool table. And there's a one-lane bowling alley off to the side, though I've never seen anybody use it.

The stage is not even a foot high, and the piano is not a piano, just a Casio keyboard connected to a fizzing amp from the '90s. And there's a microphone and a music stand for the vocalists. The program is a single photocopied sheet of paper with everyone's name listed beside the piece they are going to perform. At the top it says: *Debbie's School of Music—Music for All Ages!* and the *S* in *School* is a treble clef. My piano teacher, Roxy, is the MC, and she calls everyone up when it's their turn and thanks them when they're done.

For my costume this year, I'm doing a David Bowie tribute, and I know I worked too hard on it when I should have been practising. My sister put the two-tone lightning bolt across my face, the right angle and colour, so it cuts completely over my closed eye and then zigzags over the bridge of my nose. And I have the red-dye hairspray and the sequined shirt. Halloween is my favourite holiday by far, and I always try to pull together something good, but people almost never know who I am or what I'm going for.

The audience is mostly family—parents and siblings and grandparents—and then fifty or sixty of the residents. I think maybe half these people have the capacity to pay attention and take in the show. The others sit very still, usually strapped in, and it's like they are looking hard at something in the middle distance that the rest of us can't see. The spry ones come down on their own power, a few of them using walkers with hollowed-out tennis balls on the feet, and it's mostly women, sets of friends sitting together and gossiping, and maybe two or three couples that are still together. The others are wheeled in by the staff and some have oxygen tanks strapped to the backs of their chairs. There are clear tubes, very thin, that run up from the canister, then behind the ears, over the top lips, and into little pokers for each nostril.

One of the ladies has a stuffed toy in her lap, a black and white cat, and she pets him all the time.

"It's going to be okay," I heard her whisper to the animal as they brought her in.

"Next we have Catherine," Roxy says. "And she is going to give us her rendition of 'Merrily We Roll Along.'"

Catherine is seven, I think, but already an operator. She has on a tuque with pipe-cleaner antennae and a red-and-white polka-dot turtleneck with eight arms made of stuffed extra-long socks sewn into the sides and connected to one another with nearly invisible thread. Before she does her piece, Catherine bows and waves one human hand at us, and this gets the four other arms on that side waving too. When she plays, she is wearing black dollar-store gloves on her real hands, and the same gloves are on all her insect hands, so the full eight are bouncing in time as we roll along.

Roxy always says that when you take your final bow, you are recognizing the audience, thanking them, not the other way around. A bow is an acknowledgment of the connection you share. Catherine does it perfectly, natural and quick and sincere. She is not like the others, the boys who came before: an incredibly average Hulk in one of those Walmart garbage-bag getups, and then two thunderless Thors.

"Thank God for the little spider or the ladybug or whatever she's supposed to be. That's the only one of them worth anything."

One old lady says this to another old lady. They are sitting behind my family, but talking too loud and everyone can hear.

"Yes," the other woman says. "I don't know why we bother. The fat one over there in the blue? Did you hear that? Just awful."

I scan the list and the chairs in front of me and look at who is left. A couple of cats, some vague zombies, a Frankenstein, and a few more lazy kids who play hockey and are now "dressed up" as hockey players.

The order of performers runs in reverse order of age or ability, and I am second last. Me, then Avery Brainbridge for the finale.

Avery is two years younger than me, but he has also always been at least two levels higher than me for my entire life. He is wearing white pants and white shoes and a white shirt buttoned all the way to the top, but this is just his regular recital gear, not a costume. The program says he is going to play a fugue by Bach.

I don't even know what a *fugue* is, but I know Avery will have it mastered. He wouldn't be here if he wasn't ready.

I look at him and I wonder about fugues and all the other musical terms I don't understand. Then I decide. This is the last time I am going to be second last. After today, after this, I am going to quit.

It's possible this is just a bad selection for me. The wrong song at the wrong time. "The Entertainer" is supposed to have this special ragtime bounce and there must be a trick that lets you keep your left hand beating at one tempo down on the low end while your right goes through all the rotations and little harmonic variations in the higher octaves. But I cannot get it to go.

My biggest problem is how much Roxy loves the piece, especially the pace shifts and the back-and-forth. I know she wants me to see it the way she sees it.

"I'm telling you, Darce, you can do a lot with this one," she said to me the first time she suggested it. Then she had her little history tidbit, like she does for all the pieces we choose. "When this first came out, it was such a huge hit, they used to sell copies of it on wind-up scrolls, and people would feed it straight into their player pianos."

Sometimes I imagine that's the real reason why people think they know it. Like "The Entertainer" is already spring-loaded into everyone's brain, just waiting to go off. I guess they appreciate the way it feels like it could keep running on its own forever, but to me, it just seems repetitive and relentless.

I told this to Roxy once, but she said, "No way," and pointed to a section on page 3. "Look right here. Plenty of room here for you to do your own thing and improvise for a couple of bars."

Roxy says the standards are the standards for a reason and the great composers always know exactly what they're doing. Jazz, classical, blues. She went through the music program at St. FX, and I think she maybe even has her master's. And she is in a band that plays all over town. Roxy and the Midnight Soul Machine. I see their black-and-white photocopied posters on power poles and outside bars or on the grocery store bulletin board.

On the poster, Roxy has stage make-up, maybe even glitter, on her face, and I think she is wearing a golden dress and her hair is big and her eyes are closed and her mouth is open as wide as it can go. Like in those classic shots of Aretha or Etta James. Roxy's fist is clenched and her head is tilted way back and over to the side of the mic. The horn section is behind her and the trombone guy has his arm fully extended and the drummer is caught with both sticks in the air. Even though the poster is stuck beside business cards for dog groomers and landscapers, you can still feel the way the band is all together on this one note and belting it out.

She doesn't look like that when I'm with her. During our lessons, she is just herself, sweatshirt and jeans, and waiting on the bench in one of the little practice rooms at Debbie's.

We picked the song about a month ago, and we've been chunking it bit by bit. Breaking it down to its hardest sections and trickiest fingerings. Roxy points to the pages and then to the keys.

"Gonna get rough around here," she says. "But don't worry. We can smooth it out."

She writes notes directly on my sheets, and we decide where I should be by next week.

"I need you to meet me right here," she says, and there is an arrow and an exclamation mark and a star at the bottom of the fourth page.

When we're pushed up against each other on the bench, it seems easy enough, and I always think I should be able to get to where she needs me to be in seven days. But it's never the same at home by myself. When I'm alone, and I'm trying but I can't get it to work, sometimes it feels like the music itself, the actual sheets, are making fun of me.

What is wrong with you? they ask.

It wasn't always like this. I used to be good. At home, I have three first-place certificates and two seconds from Kiwanis competitions. Avery is the only person from Debbie's who has ever done better.

I don't know what happened. Sometimes I think I'm actually losing it, like there are connections inside my head that aren't working right anymore, and whatever skill I used to have is seeping out of me. I feel like I can barely hold on to anything anymore. Can't read a book, can't listen to the teacher in school, can't be fully there for Roxy when she's trying her best to show me a way though all these circles and dots and lines and flags.

People tell me it's nothing: "Just a stage," they say. "It's going to be okay."

But I would like a better explanation. Like something from a textbook or a manual, a page that an expert could point to and say: "Right here, Darcy. This is the problem and this is how we're going to fix it." Maybe a basic ADHD diagnosis, like everyone else seems to have. Or one of those low-dose social anxiety disorders.

At school, it feels like there's a whole squad of education experts and guidance counsellors sniffing around for these conditions, but they never caught a whiff of anything coming off me. I had to set up the appointments myself, and I answered all their questions while they wrote their notes, but that was as far as I got. Everyone was just kind and patient and supportive, but none of them were handing out prescriptions or giving me a special journal-writing program to follow.

"Let's check back in a couple of months, Darcy," one of the doctors told me. We were sitting in two chairs facing each other and she leaned in close. "I know it seems impossible sometimes, but I think you're going to get through just fine."

I nodded when she said this, and I may have even managed to smile, but I cannot tell you how shitty it felt to hear those words.

I used to be able to sit at a piano for hours, just fooling around and finding a melody and making my own patterns. The keyboard used to be like the computer; a whole afternoon, a week of afternoons could disappear into it. Now my mom has me wired directly to the stove timer.

"Please," she says. "Just give me twenty minutes. Come on." And the blue numbers start counting down, but I can never make it all the way.

When today is over and I am truly done, that will be seven years at Debbie's, the last three all steady with Roxy. Seven years of lessons, but I don't have much to show. I can read and I can count, yes, but not great. Just enough to get by. And we do a page of theory every week. If you put a basic selection in front of me, I can give you a version of it, but I know I'm way behind the kids who really practise. I'm way behind where I could be.

In the Brookfield audience, my parents and my sister are sitting with me and I know this is going to be hard for them too. I stayed up too late last night, trying to cram, and nobody got any sleep, and this morning I started making whole new kinds of mistakes, even with the easiest stuff, the sections I used to have down.

There's one sequence, where the melody folds in on itself before it surges again into a new voice, but it's impossible. The bars are all numbered, and my problems have been underlined and circled three or four times. Week after week, Roxy uses a different colour ink. But it's like there's a disconnect between my mind and my fingers, and I just cannot hit those keys on the beat and in the right order.

If you had the music in front of you, I could show you the exact spot. "Wait right here," I'd say, "and you'll see what happens."

Maybe an hour ago, my dad listened to me half-assing my way through it for the two hundredth time. He stood there, about a foot behind me, and didn't say anything. Just watched me crash the car, again and again. The same place every time, the fold and then the surge, a turn I cannot turn.

"You know we're paying for this, don't you?" he eventually said. "It's not free. Your mother and I. We keep paying and paying, but I don't know exactly what it is that we're buying anymore."

My parents don't play anything and they are not music people and it's not their dream to see me in a concert hall. They just don't want me to embarrass myself. And they don't like it when I'm "squandering an opportunity" or wasting other people's time.

"What about Avery Brainbridge?" my mother asked me once, even though she knows how much I hate it when she does comparisons. "Do you think *he* needs a stove timer to get him to practise? And Roxy. Don't you ever wonder what Roxy thinks about all of this?"

ROXY

What you think about all of this is that people who really know things, experts, should be allowed to tell the truth.

At least once, you would like to put your finger on the note, right on the dot, and tell someone that *that* is not how it goes.

"No, Krista, that is objectively wrong."

Or, "Look at what it says, Matthew. Read. The. Music. Actually read it."

Or, "Just listen, Rebecca. Listen to yourself. Do you honestly think it is supposed to sound like that?"

Ten minutes late for class is the standard. A third of thirty minutes already gone and nothing to do but hope it won't stretch to twenty and a cancellation. You keep checking the phone for a text or a quick email update, a little basic courtesy. Refresh and refresh, five times in a minute, then more waiting, alone on your half of the bench, in front of another crappy keyboard, behind another hollow plastic door.

It should be illegal and it probably is, Debbie's policy on this stuff. If a student doesn't show up and they don't pay for a lesson they didn't take, then she just passes the loss down the line and you don't get your money.

But what is a person supposed to do? Where can you go for a "free" half-hour in the middle of a teaching line? The room is a cell. If you stand and extend your arms, you can touch the front and back walls at the same time.

Most of them do make it eventually. At 7:42, the next French immersion girl arrives with her iPad and her earbuds, still wearing her soccer uniform and her shin guards. She tosses a Subway wrapper into the garbage can and wipes the mayo off her face.

Debbie has her business model figured out and she knows her people: the stretched-out and overcommitted. Parents and kids going through the motions. They can't focus on anything, so they don't really expect any progress.

"Sorry, Roxy," this girl, Amber, says, looking down at her running shoes as she talks. "Didn't really get a chance to practise this week."

"That's okay," you tell her. "Why don't you just show me what you do have."

The only one you have any hope for is Darcy. Darcy and maybe Catherine. But she is too young and maybe he is too old. You know how it goes. Right around here, somewhere between twelve and fifteen, that's when they usually quit. But you thought he was different—you *know* Darcy is different—so you pushed him a bit and you made him take on "The Entertainer" even though it was clear he didn't want to do it. You hoped the challenge, the middle part, fast and technical, would light him up again and bring him back across the line, over here to your side of the world. Maybe the kid was only slipping a bit, but not completely gone. Not yet.

Now, though, you're not so sure. Maybe you're the one who made the mistake, and when this is all over, he is going to end up on the other side with the rest of them. You think about it all the time. What it used to be like when you were around that age. The practice schedule you had to keep. Up at six for ninety minutes before school and two hours afterwards. Doubled on the weekends. Twelve years old and warming up your fingers every morning, and then, all through the day at school, feeling that stiffness in your back and your shoulders and your neck. The way your teachers, Mrs. Jeannie Cargill first, then Daniel, then Ingrid, pushed so hard it even scared your parents. The upper levels of the Royal Conservatory curriculum, 7, 8, and 9. Formal examinations, usually in June, and the cold winter recitals in silent university halls. All the music people from your childhood with their dark clothes and their judgments. Some of them were great, but a lot them were not.

But you don't know anymore. Maybe that way was just as bad, or even worse than what Debbie is doing to these families: taking their money and giving them nothing in exchange. It feels impossible sometimes. You approach the same problem from two opposite directions and still end up with the same garbage results. When you were Darcy's age, remember, you once counted out twenty-five extra-strength Tylenols and lined them up on your dresser before sweeping them into your palm. And you had a can of orange Crush right there and ready to go. You stared into your palm and imagined them like a fistful of Tic Tacs. Shove, chew, drink, swallow. Enough for a good stomach pumping. That was the plan. Just sick enough to skip the grade 7 exam. But even back then, you knew it wouldn't work. You thought about what people would think. What they would say.

Never any risk of that at Debbie's. The parents, scattered and apathetic, keep bringing their children back, and your job is only to run the conveyor and slide them along. Thirty-five dollars for half an hour of Bastien 1, 2, 3 and the whole Christopher Norton catalogue. As long as everybody shows up and does their part, thirty-five dollars for every half an hour (eight to the actual teacher), it almost runs itself.

Debbie's School of Music is really just the main floor of a low-income house that she bought for nothing and chopped into eight drywalled practice rooms. Piano and guitar mostly, and vocal, and a Cape Breton fiddle run twice a week. There are two leatherette sofas for the people who have to wait, and a bathroom that really should be cleaned by a professional. Then eight hollow doors and eight little rooms with eight professionally trained people like you waiting inside.

Debbie rents out the upstairs apartment for another revenue stream, but who could possibly live there? No soundproofing and the vocal kids sending in the clowns every night and Celine Dion's heart going on and on.

The money is just barely okay. Sixteen dollars an hour, sure, but there are not nearly enough hours. This is the music business, you tell yourself. Technically speaking, you are still in the music business. Playing and singing and getting paid for it. Living off your art, your sole source of income.

When people ask "What do you do?," you say, "I teach Monday to Thursday, and then we take the Machine on the road for the weekends."

But that isn't entirely right. It isn't every weekend, and you don't go very far. Two standing shows you can count on, Bearly's House of Blues every other Friday, and the Company House once a month. Then whatever else you can scrounge. Maybe Truro or the Island three times a year. Or one good university show per term in Wolfville or Antigonish or Moncton. Anything to get through the winter and into the tourist season and when the festival circuit starts running and you might get to talk with real programmers who have real budgets.

The Machine is always saving up for more studio time and rehearsing whenever you can get everyone's schedule to work out. Mostly in the basement of your trumpet player, Lyle. All your coats piled up on the dryer and the furnace always cutting in. The Machine has six quality originals, bar tested and ready to put down. That is two-thirds of a record.

"Why Don't You Come On Over to Me?," a song you wrote, is already a classic. Some nights the crowd even calls for it and, most of the time now, the Machine holds it back for the encore. If you could come up with three more like "Come On Over," the album might have a chance. But you haven't written anything in a year and a half, and if it is ever going to happen it has got to happen soon. Damien, your drummer, has options and you know he is thinking about them harder than he should.

"Look around, Rox," he told you last week. He had his kit set up by Lyle's freezer. "We can't keep going like this forever."

Damien is the best drummer in Nova Scotia; no, the best drummer in the Maritime provinces, and maybe the best you have ever seen, up close, in real life. Ask anyone who knows anything. Ask them about the rhythm section of the Midnight Soul Machine. Damien Coolis and Carlos Rodriguez on bass. The narrow spaces those two negotiate with each other, the way they never miss. Every single show, Damien is back there holding everything down, and you think nothing good can start until he counts it in. But everybody else can see it too. The Slickers, indie folk rockers from the Halifax side of the harbour, a band with too many words and too much whining for your taste, signed their deal a few months ago and it has turned out to be real. Now they have a full cross-country tour lined up, even Quebec. Shows every other day, already booked and paid for, and they didn't have to do any of it themselves.

And of course, there is something else you don't want to lose with Dame. Half a dozen hookups that came around only when that was absolutely the right thing to do. Late at night, and the buzz of the show still clinging to you, the energy of the crowd still flowing, and this opening right here. The way you both knew exactly when it was time to go and exactly what should be happening next and next and next right on to the end. With Damien, sometimes you think, because you play music, the two of you share a connection that is important and serious, and when you come together after a show, that's not the same as when you do it with other people. But it can only work if you are both in the Machine.

Some nights when you are up there, out front, between the kit and the crowd, you can feel the beat coming from the back and passing through your body and out to the people. The bass drum steady and hard, and how easy it seems to be, for Damien, to find that balance and ride it. Sitting on his stool, working both pedals, his knees pounding, like it is his job to pump all the air into this room and keep everyone alive. And his wrists rolling over everything he has to touch in that precise half second. Then Carlos, *boom*, *boom*, *boom*, *boom*, then Lyle and the horns, then maybe just a couple rhythm chords from you on the keyboard, and the guitar. And your voice, not really on top, but usually inside of it, right where it needs to be. Sound-checked and the mix you wanted coming back through the monitors.

The Machine has its crowd, loyal followers who never miss a show. They come in two main varieties: The people who like to dance, going for it every night, out on the floor from the first to the last, sweating even harder than you. And then the people who prefer to sit, always at the same tables, really listening and nodding their heads. Almost nobody talks when the Machine is running. You love that so much.

And, yes, there is a plan, a setlist, but it doesn't have to go that way. The Machine can read a room and push harder or dial it back.

Carlos makes those calls. He watches the faces and how the bodies are moving. When one song is winding down, he may walk around the stage and lock eyes with every member of the band.

"All over?" he asks. "Right now?"

Like everyone else, you nod and you smile because his suggestions always work.

When it's just yourselves after rehearsal, down by the washing machine and the freezer, sometimes somebody will pull up Stevie Wonder's *Songs in the Key of Life* on their phone and let it shuffle, and you'll just listen or play along for little sections. Any spot will do. The 1976 double album and the bonus EP, every track, every second. Two full hours.

There are deep cuts you would like to share—"As," "Another Star," "Saturn"—but during the show, you have to kill, so you stick to what the crowd recognizes and feed them only the hits.

The horns and the cymbals at the top of "Sir Duke."

You have been in arguments about this. Maybe the best opening Stevie Wonder ever wrote.

Lyle and Dame and Carlos and your voice.

The simple joy of a well-executed cover. Sometimes, you can't believe how easy it is. A bar band just needs to get out of the way and give the people what they want. You go through two verses and one chorus, then you point the mic at the audience and hold it above their heads. A hundred bodies in front of you, waving their hands and shaking their asses.

"Everybody now," you call out, but sometimes you think you're too obvious. Maybe they can hear the pleading in your voice.

There's no need to worry, though. He laid this down fifty years ago, and it still works like new. All these people, they feel it. Immediately and all over. You think about it more than you should: the link between you and the Machine and this crowd and the music that Stevie Wonder worked out in 1976. Nothing else feels like this.

The only problem is you don't like beer. Especially not draft beer and especially not as a from of currency. Payment in exchange for services rendered. You know it's just as tight for the bar own-ers as it is for you, but God. They see you arriving four hours before the show and they watch you bringing in the gear, and they know it's rented, and for sure they see there are still seven of you.

Two hundred and fifty dollars, divided by seven, every other Friday, and whatever you can get at the door. And three pitchers of house draft, something below Bud Light and only available here. The very last name at the bottom of the chalkboard. Horse Power or Boot Liquor, a name like that. This is what you get. Three pitchers of Horse Power, divided by seven. And you are on from ten till two. And on your own for all those gin and tonics.

Last night you looked back at Damien, crashing both cym-bals at the same time, and you saw it coming. A time after he had moved on. His disinterested face staring out of The Slickers' curated feed, and their slick website with all their slick merch and their long line of upcoming dates, and the rest of you following him now only on Instagram. And the record never completed, untitled and stuck at six tracks forever. And the remnants of the Machine—maybe just you and Carlos and Lyle and a bunch of fill-ins, strangers you could halfway teach the parts to—standing together on the side of the road, changing a tire at the base of Kelly's Mountain on the way to Sydney. You turned your head and you thought you could see the future, but you cannot let it happen.

So you got up this morning. And you made the copies. Debbie's son has a hockey tournament so she can't come to the recital, but she will pay a full six-hour block if you do the set-up and tear-down at Brookfield and MC the concert. It's Halloween and you thought about throwing together a bare minimum costume, your reliable Raggedy Ann go-to, but in the end, you couldn't be bothered. So now you are up here looking exactly like what you are.

Beside you, Cindy sends in the clowns again, nodding her head when they are finally here. The blood vessels in your dehydrated brain pound and there is an extra-salty taste in your mouth. At first you imagine it as a joke—the master of cer-emonies from Debbie's School of Music puking on a child's shoes while she gives it her all in the recital—but then you feel it rising for real, a surging sludge of pizza and gin, and you have to turn your back and cover your mouth and choke it down, this toxic, almost solid burp.

You have been crossing the names off the list, and you look up and see him there, Darcy, in the crowd with his family. It is his turn. Fifteen per cent of these kids haven't come at all and part of you wonders why Darcy didn't just join that crowd and bail on this one and live to try again another time. Another part of you loves him, you realize this now. You must love this boy if only because you hate so much what is about to happen to him. He has been with you for three years—every week, always early, and, at least until recently, always ready to go. And he is the best student you ever had at Debbie's, a former Kiwanis champion. But you feel like everyone is leaving now—giving up and moving on.

"Now we have Darcy," you say.

His eyes are closed and his head is down, but when you say his name, he looks up and you lock eyes for a second before he blinks his lightning bolt, long and slow, and stands. He seems completely alone.

"Darcy is a great, great piano player." You want to make sure this goes out through the microphone. "And he is going to give us his version of 'The Entertainer.' "

He makes his way sideways down the row, past his family and the zombies and the Power Rangers, then straight up the middle aisle. You watch the audience turning and trying to take him in. *That is David Bowie right there*, you think. Nearly perfectly executed.

You see him walking and you notice the way they don't recognize him, and it makes you wonder, again, about all the things people don't know they don't know. As he strides past the end of her row, one of the older ladies recoils in disgust and actually pulls away from him. She makes a face and waves her hand at him dismissively.

"Can anybody tell me," she asks, too loud, "why not a single kid on this planet can be a normal person anymore?"

GLADYS FERGUSON'S HUSBAND

They come down because it is the weekend, and this is the only programming option for today. Something different. Whenever he can, he likes to cultivate a good disruption, anything that might push her out of her last quiet loop. She has not said a word in three days—a long time, but not the longest they've been through—and he thinks maybe the change of scenery will help. He dresses her and clicks on the electric toothbrush and moves the little vibrating head inside her mouth, front to back. The same thing every morning. The doctors say this part is supposed to stay routine. Teeth, then hair. She loves the feel of the brush going through again and again, running all the way down to the end of the strand.

Then earrings. A different pair every day. He pushes the metal posts through the holes and goes behind to attach the fasteners.

She is sitting down, and they both look at themselves in the same mirror. When he holds up a tube of lipstick, she puckers up.

"That's my girl," he says.

Then shuffling into the hall. This is his goal. Keep her up, keep her walking for as long as he can. The woman once ran a marathon, for God's sake. He does not want her stuck in a chair for the rest of her life. They ride the elevator down to the common area and take seats in the very front row. He says hello and she nods at the nurses and some of the people they used to play cards with, but he knows there is nothing behind it. A real game-changer is what he's after, something way, way out of the ordinary. In the last year, he's found that only a profound distraction can trip the familiar synapse and light the light. Then she will come out for a little while, out and back. Maybe just a wink, or a raised eyebrow, or a tilt of her head, but he'll see her in there, the old troublemaker.

Sounds are even better. If somebody drops a glass in the dining area, the shattering will make her turn her head. "What *is* that?" she will say to him, perfectly clear. As though the noise is an interruption, cutting into a long conversation they are no longer having.

For the last year, he has been keeping up both sides of their exchanges.

"I see the music kids are here again," he told her this morning. "Maybe we'll check them out. What would you say to that?"

She massaged her cheek, then pulled on her right ear.

"Very good," he said. "Sounds like a plan."

She used to play the piano a little bit. Some lessons when she was a kid, long before he met her, but it was always a surprise for him, how much she retained. They had an old never-tuned, barely touched Heintzman in their dining room, really just a shelf for plants and family pictures. If the table got too crowded at Thanksgiving, they might rest a few side dishes of mashed potatoes or turnip up there. But once a year, during their Christmas party, she would fold back the top and pull their one music book out of the bench and run through the carols. Just chords and some melody. Enough to accompany someone singing "Jolly Old Saint Nicholas," and "I'm Getting Nothing," and "Ode to Joy." Even "Good King Wenceslas," somehow.

When they chose this place only five years ago, they walked in together, straight through the sliding doors, pulling their own rolling suitcases behind them. Both in their early eighties, but still on their feet and, he felt, well ahead of everybody else they knew. Even though they were completely surrounded by the condition—it had had taken one of their best friends, early onset, when the man was barely sixty—they still didn't see it coming. She used to read a book a day—mysteries and true crime and slutty romances—boxes of them every month, picked up and dropped off at church sales.

Their first unit had been fine, just a regular apartment with almost everything from the old place, except all on one level. And a full-sized proper kitchen so they could cook whatever they wanted, even invite people over, and a reserved parking spot close to the door. They were free to leave whenever they liked.

They enjoyed it for the first while, but he could never quite shake the knowledge that they had sold their real house to get in here, and now there were other, younger people sleeping in their bedroom, and staring at their fireplace, and not taking care of the hedges or the garden in the right way.

He tried to be positive for her sake. Tried not to feel like they were now always going to be "visitors," or "guests," or "residents" in a place where they were supposed to live forever. It was easier for her. She was always looking ahead, planning trips. When the grandchildren came the first time, she toured them around like it was a resort.

"Wait till you see!" she told them.

Then down to the pool and over to the little theatre space where you could make a reservation and show whatever movie you wanted on the big screen. And ice cream from the soft-serve machine in the dining room. She swept them through all of it in an hour. Eighty years old and still wearing people out. Even bowled a strike. Two hands, sure, and not too fast, but right down the middle of the lane and all the pins falling over.

Of course, it was costing them everything. The house money in the bank, their pensions, and something extra from their emergency fund, but he knew the numbers could only run in the other direction now. In the first weeks, he found himself calculating almost continuously. How much for how long? Whole years of their past savings exchanged for just a few weeks and months in the present. He was pretty sure they could almost make it, get through without having to burden the kids. But then the step-ups started—really, he thought they should be called step-downs—and there was a different pricing package for each one of them. They had to keep moving.

First over to C wing, where Brookfield ran its "Memory Assistance Program," then all the way down to D and the full "Enriched Care and Security" package. Buzzers and magnetic locks on every door, regular nursing visits and hygiene checks, and signing in and out for every little thing. Guards and extra staff everywhere. Cleaning people with keys that opened every single room and every single drawer. Strangers coming in whenever they wanted, digging through their stuff.

When they finally arrived here, in the heart of D, he'd had to sign over everything to his oldest daughter, including power of attorney, and he knew all four of the kids were now kicking in as much as they could to make it work. He refused to ask anyone for the total, but he knew it was a number that could not be sustained.

She was not allowed near a stove anymore, not even a toaster, and the bathroom was full of risks. And her diet had to be monitored more closely, bland food on a bland schedule, and he could barely get a cup of coffee when he wanted it. Though he didn't need any of this attention himself, he had followed her down through every stage. There was no way they could afford him taking up a single room in A while she was over here. And he needed to be close to her. That was the real truth. He couldn't accept not being close to her. The only other option would be to turn her over to the province, which meant you had no choice and no control at all. Whatever room opened up first, that's where they would send her, no matter where it was.

He knew women in Halifax with husbands lost in Yarmouth or Cape Breton. They saw each other maybe once a month now, if they were lucky. Their friends were always asking him to drive. Could he leave her for the day and run them down to Yarmouth, three hours each way? Though they knew he was not comfortable anymore, driving on the highway or at night.

It had started at the garden centre. They used to have a little plot, one of the community beds in the Dartmouth Commons. Five rows of tomatoes and cucumbers and some lettuce and flowers. They put a fence around it and stepping stones so they could move through without disturbing anything. It was not like their old yard, but big enough and always changing. Something to keep them busy.

They had all the gear in the trunk: buckets and trowels and Miracle-Gro, hats and gloves, and bug spray and sunscreen. And they brought their own lawn chairs, and often a picnic, and they used to sit out for a few hours on the sunny afternoons with the people from the community pizza oven. She loved the mix. Chatting with everyone about their different secrets for the crusts and the sauces, or just humming to herself and weeding.

But then one day when they were at the Kent Building Supplies on Baker Drive, surveying their options and wandering past the pallets piled high with mulch and black earth and wood chips, he selected an envelope of seeds off the rack and held it over his shoulder. He thought she was right there with him, a half-step behind.

"What do you think about this?" he asked, but when he turned around, he could not find her.

At first he wasn't overly concerned. The store was massive and packed with gadgets and curiosities. He thought some distraction had caught hold of her and she would catch up soon enough. So he turned back to the rack and considered the other possibilities. Every envelope had a photograph that showed what would happen to these seeds if they were cultivated in the perfect light and the perfect heat and the perfect soil.

But after fifteen minutes, when she still had not come back, he started to worry. He went slowly at first, trying his best to stay calm as he ambled down the one wide corridor in the middle while he glanced left and right down the narrower aisles, even electrical and plumbing, though he knew she would not be there.

After another half an hour, when she still wasn't anywhere to be found, not in the women's bathroom—he checked under every stall—and nowhere inside the entire metal shell of the warehouse, he knew that he had arrived at a meridian in his life, and things on the other side would never be the same.

As the customer service person made the announcement, he listened to her name coming out of the speakers and bouncing off the walls. It already sounded far away and unfamiliar, and he imagined how others in the store would think of her only as a stranger.

"Gladys Ferguson. Gladys Ferguson. Would Gladys Ferguson

please come to the front checkout. Your husband is looking for you."

Then security, then a sweep of the parking lot, then the police. They had already received calls about a woman strolling in the median of the Circumferential Highway while six lanes of traffic surged around her at 120 kilometres an hour.

When they picked her up, she had bunches of dandelions in both her hands and stuffed into her pockets. Everything pulled out all the way to the roots. "Are you seeing these weeds?" she asked the officers. "Pretty bad, but I think we can still make it nice."

Then the descent. It felt like every month something else would go. Slowly, all the words for all the objects faded away. First *rubber boots*, then *blender*, then *television*.

"Hey there, what would you call this now?" she asked him, waving a spoon in his face.

Then their kids' names, then his.

She bit him once, so hard it broke the skin and he had to hide the marks from the staff. And then another time, she punched a woman in the chest just for walking too close to them in the hall. They'd been called in for that one, and officially written up, a letter inserted into their file.

But on that same day, in the middle of a TV show, she turned to him and started giving detailed instructions for Percy, their dog from forty years ago. "I swear to God, I don't know why we even have him if they aren't going to take care of him. Whose turn was it today? Can somebody tell me that?"

—

Perhaps this had been a mistake. The crowd was bigger than he'd anticipated, and he hadn't prepared himself for the costumes. Maybe the scene was too far out of the ordinary to be helpful. And, objectively, the children were not doing a good job. Except for the spider. He felt sure that even the MC was not impressed. She seemed to be rolling her eyes at the vocalists especially, but he could not disagree. When they sang, the kids closed their eyes and circled their hands in the air, aiming for notes they could not possibly hit. Around him, people visibly winced, and when it was over, they applauded the quiet and not what had come before.

He surveyed the program. Two left. "The Entertainer" and a fugue. He did not know what that was.

An adolescent boy in tight jeans and face paint took his half-step up onto the stage, about five feet away from them. He gave a slight bow and spread out his sheets, then positioned his fingers in the right spot. At first there was nothing, a long pause, then a little run down the keyboard from the right to the left, and just the beginning of the most famous part, then nothing again.

The boy took his hands off the keyboard and folded them in his lap and stared at them hard. He gave a long exhale and continued to sit still with his chin lowered so far it touched his chest. Then he seemed to shudder, and he glanced over his shoulder at the MC.

It went on too long. He thought: *Either this is part of it, or it is not part of it.* Sometimes you can't tell the difference between what is a mistake and what is on purpose. He studied it more intensely, this scene unfolding in front of him. A motionless boy sitting at a piano making no sound. Every next second seemed more pressurized, slowed down and sped up at the same time, and he didn't know exactly what was happening.

DARCY

I don't know exactly what is happening. I go down through the first three bars, not fast, and I start the start, but then there is nothing else, not even the simple first sections, the parts I really do know, all the lines I used to have. Everything slows down and then it stops, and I see myself being seen by all these people. I take my fingers off the keys and study my hands, but it is as though they belong to someone else now, and I don't think I can order them around anymore. I turn to my sheets. *What is wrong with you?* they ask again. *Everybody else can do this.*

Then I glance over my shoulder and try to find Roxy.

"It's going to be okay," she whispers.

In the crowd, I see the masks and the hockey players and Frankenstein and my parents, my dad shaking his head. And little Catherine with her antennae up. She looks like she is about to cry, and I think this is because of me. I knew what was coming and I have already imagined every one of these details, but I think that only makes it worse, the fact I'm so prepared. Like the slowest bullet ever was fired at my head more than a month ago, and I saw it coming, another foot every couple of days, and now, even when the metal tip is pressed up against the bridge of my nose, I still can't get out of the way.

There is nothing left to do, so I breathe out for the last time and get ready to leave. This is how it ends.

But then, right in front of me—and I mean right, right in front of me, so close she blocks out everything else—an older, well-dressed lady stands up.

Her hair is parted precisely, and she is wearing earrings and makeup and lipstick.

She gets up, and she is straight and tall, and there is clarity in her eyes, aimed just at me and this piano and this song. It only takes her two steps to cross over.

One: away from the old man beside her. He looks scared and surprised, and I see how he reaches out to grab her, but it is too late.

Then two: up the half step and onto the stage and over to me. She puts her hand on my shoulder and gestures with her head.

"Move over," she says.

ROXY

Even when you see things happening, sometimes you still don't know what's happening. Or what you're supposed to do about it. You watch Darcy breaking down, stalling like that in front of everyone. Hands in his lap and chin on his chest. Everything in the room has stopped, and yet all you want is for *this* to stop.

He looks at his sheets, then glances over his shoulder, and you feel the way he is searching for you.

"It's going to be okay," you say.

But even as the line comes out of your mouth, you hear how empty it sounds. Your grade 7 adjudicator used the exact same words, just before she had to fail you. It doesn't matter that you were miles ahead of Darcy's material when it happened. You were around this age, and the moment paralyzed you in the same way. You'd been preparing for the exam for a year, and you had it down, but in the room, when it was time to go, you couldn't even get to your études or the repertoire. Instead, you lost it right from the beginning, at the technical section, where it's only scales and arpeggios.

The examiner thought she was giving you an easy one.

"Can you show me the formula pattern for D-minor harmonic?"

It was nothing, but also way too much, and it seemed like the room was tipping and now you were falling backwards off the bench. You couldn't talk and you shook your head, and you know now that the examiner understood the situation right away.

"It's going to be okay," she said. "How about the chromatic scale starting at G-flat?"

Another no.

It was just the two of you in the room and there was no audience, but it felt like everyone you'd ever known was there, watching this happen. The examiner tried a few more times— "The dominant seventh of F-major broken?"—then she put her hand on your shoulder and stood up and quietly went to the door to call in your parents.

"I think Roxanne is just having a hard day," she said.

That moment and this moment combine. The boy is only a few feet away, and you are the master of ceremonies: you are supposed to be in charge. An action is required, and you know you should be the one to put your hand on his shoulder. Maybe step in front and shield him from these people.

But before you can move, an old lady, one of the residents, not a parent, steps onto the stage.

"Move over," she tells him.

You see the stunned expression on Darcy's face, but he scooches over and makes room for her. She sits down to his left, in the spot you normally occupy, and she picks up the boy's hands and positions them two octaves up. You watch Darcy watching her and you see her fingers resting over his, the way your hands sometimes touch Darcy's hands. The woman's fingers on top, then the boy's in the middle, then the keys.

She points at the music with her other hand. The treble clef and the bass.

"I'll do this," she says, "and you do that."

GLADYS FERGUSON'S HUSBAND

She is gone before he can move, and he does not know what is happening. There have been flashes like this before—surprises—but not for at least a year. Once, when they were watching the news, a wave moved through her and she got up off the couch, grabbed the remote control, pushed the red button to turn everything off, and threw it on the floor.

"I have had enough," she said, "and I want to go to bed."

He knows he should pull her back down to her seat, put her in her place, but when he looks to the boy, he can tell the child is not scared. Gladys, the real Gladys, used to be unstoppable, defiant in these kinds of situations. Nothing made her more furious than witnessing another person suffer embarrassment. He remembers how she once elbowed her way to the front of the line at the grocery store. A thin woman was stuck at the register with a screaming kid in a cart and the bags already loaded. The woman had cash in her hand but not enough, and the checkout clerk was slowly going through the receipt, one item at a time, and looking in the bags, trying to find the things that had to be returned to make this work.

They were maybe five carts back and everybody else was just watching it happen.

"Will you *please* excuse me," Gladys said as she shoved past with her wallet out and the credit card held up. "I need to get through."

The way her hands touch the boy's hands, the way she points at the music. He feels certain it will not turn violent. Or this is his certain hope. He knows things can change so quickly.

The teacher, the master of ceremonies, is right there too. And he can sense that she is ready like he is. Both crouched on either side of the stage, both coiled and ready to spring into action if this moment starts to turn in the wrong direction. But that is not how it appears to be going. For now, at least, they wait and let the scene continue to play out on its own. They want to see what is going to happen.

"I'll do this, and you do that," Gladys says, and all her words and all her meanings connect. "You, there, and me, here."

The boy nods his lightning bolt head and Gladys Ferguson's husband checks the program again.

Darcy MacIntyre—"The Entertainer"

He doesn't know who this kid is, but the man can tell he understands.

DARCY

I do not know who this woman is, but I understand her plan right away. Sometimes it can just click like that. Another person comes along, and they deliver the message in a slightly different way and now the whole thing makes sense. I know how to do it. The ragtime beat, call and reply. Just doubled up or maybe divided by two. I look ahead, through the whole five pages, and I can see all the exchanges that are coming. We have never met, and I cannot tell you her name, but we know the parts we have to play, and how the rest will go.

I nod my head and we begin. The first bars are still the first bars, and I run it down from my side of the piano one more time, setting her up perfectly. But now there's no longer any reason to stop. I can hold on to the tempo and speak the high notes to her, while she bounces the chords and takes care of the bottom end and talks back to me from the lower registers. For the first time, I think I see it the way Scott Joplin saw it, or maybe I hear it the way he must have heard it, more than a hundred years ago, before any of this was ever written down and "The Entertainer" was just a pattern of silent sounds swirling inside his head.

ROXY

You see it the same way they see it. Or the same way the well-dressed woman saw it when she was still a member of the audience. This is a solution. And you know it is going to work for Darcy because it has always worked for you. It's just better, so much better, when you are not up there, up here, alone.

You remember yourself stopped in the soundproofed room with your adjudicator, and you recall how, at that moment, and for even a few days afterwards, you thought for sure this was the end of everything. But then you remember, as well, performing with your first high school band, Tempus Fugit. And the first time you were in a bar and you heard Damien Coolis on drums, and the way it woke you up. And the night the Midnight Soul Machine started running in Lyle's basement. And the first time you sang so hard you thought you might crack your own ribs.

Your brain is still thrumming from last night at the Company House, when the Horse Power flowed through the crowd, and strangers were singing your words back to you. *Why don't you come on over to me?*

It's going to be okay.

Sometimes you wonder why you are still doing this or who, exactly, you are doing it for. And then, sometimes, you don't wonder at all.

GLADYS FERGUSON'S HUSBAND

He lowers himself back into his seat in the front row, and for the first time in three years, he feels the pressure around his chest lessening a bit, and a full deep breath entering his lungs before he lets it all go. He does not need to see her face. Just that posture is enough. Straight up and down. Hips below shoulders and the relaxed certainty in her limbs. Her toes tapping and her arms extended away from her body. The way she smiles and nods at the boy. He remembers how she taught the kids to swim. Their youngest son glued to the wall of the pool. "Come on, Mr. Barnacle," she used to joke. "Let's get this thing going. You know I don't have all day."

He looks around. All these other people. You *are* seeing this, aren't you? He tries to understand his relative position. *I am with them now*, he thinks, *and we are the audience, and that, up there, is the show.* He wonders if he still exists for her, if he continues to occupy some space in her head. Probably not, he decides. She is on to something else, and I am gone.

—

THE BROOKFIELD FUGUE (STRETTO)

I look at her and you look at him and he looks at us.

And I am playing this music and she is doing it too, and you can see the song running all the way to the end.

Everyone knows how it goes.

Da . . . da . . . da-da . . . da-da . . . da-da.

She holds it down on the left and you watch her building the foundation. And I am over here on the right, spinning through the variations.

Da da . . . da-da-da-da . . . da-da . . . da.

We are all on the beat and, oh yeah, *this* is "The Entertainer."

The melody heads out, then comes back, and the high part talks to the low, and there are rotations on top of rotations on top of rotations. And just when you think the whole composition is about to disintegrate, that's when all the strands reassemble for the end.

"Yes!" Catherine yells, and she jumps up and stands on her chair, clapping all her hands at once.

The others follow. It is not over, not quite, but this is what they call an ovation. Everyone rises. Children and parents, wives and husbands, animals and insects, heroes and monsters, strangers and people who have known each other all their lives.

I am turning the turn, and we can both see the last line and you know they are going to make it home.

But then I catch something coming out of the crowd—the old man in the front row, his voice cutting in just before the finish.

You look over and he is not yelling, but the sound carries. Everyone can hear it.

"One more time," the man requests. "From the beginning."

Then a single word, repeated.

"Again," he says, and "again."

THE NINTH CONCESSION

ONCE, WHEN I WAS KID, I PIERCED MYSELF STRAIGHT through the meat of my upper arm while I was playing on the empty tobacco trailers at Allan Klassen's farm. I didn't feel it when it happened, and I'm still not exactly sure what it was that ran through me like that, so quick and surgical and clean. Most likely it was a hitch pin, or maybe one of the clasps, those twisting fasteners that slip through the hole at the bottom and connect one trailer to the next. Or it could have been an exposed nail or a scrap of sheet metal or any other random farm hazard. At that time, there were a thousand unnoticed things lying around that could seriously damage a person.

We used to ride the trailers like they were industrial-grade teeter-totters, massive fulcrums that barely registered our weight and flung our bodies around like we weren't even there. Allan and I would stand at opposite ends, maybe twenty feet apart, and take turns bending our knees as deeply as we could, then pumping hard to get them rocking. The connecting pin, or whatever it was, must have hit me while I was in full flight, going through the turnaround between the up and the down, but I can't really know for sure. The only certainty is that something very sharp, like a drill press, passed into me, then out of me, through both sides of my K-way windbreaker, and I didn't register it at all.

Allan caught it before I did.

I noticed the way his eyes came to rest on my arm and paused there for a second too long. Then how his look moved up to my face.

"You know you're a mess, right?" he said.

The blood was pooling against the nylon, down by my elbow. I reached in past the armpit and brought out my hand. It was red.

This was in the late fall. Both the corn and tobacco harvests were finished, and the killer frost had already come and gone. Everything around us, miles of empty, flattened fields, even the sky, was hollowed out and dried grey. This colour leaking out of me, alive and wet, seemed like it belonged to another season.

We both stared at my fingers, but I remember Allan's expression did not change. I could have been holding a stone or a pile of dirt in my hand, something completely separate from both of us.

"Better get it looked at," he said.

So I went to my house and he went to his.

But then I had to keep going, over to the hospital, where they gave me a tetanus shot and twelve stitches. Seven on one side of my arm and five on the other.

While we waited, I was told to sit still and apply direct pressure, but I couldn't resist the urge to examine myself. Every five minutes, I would tear back the crusting edge of the gauze and stare into the hole. A plug had been punched right through me, a perfect circle, and now I could see everything. Even a white edge of bone, halfway down.

"You know, you're a very lucky person," the doctor told me as he looped the last stitch and cut off the wire. "We could be in a very different situation here if that had hit anything important." He smoothed his hand over the sutures, admiring his work. "Instead, all we're talking about is a near miss." He put his hand on my head and ruffled my hair as he sent me through the door. "You'll be all better before you know it."

—

Allan and I were probably around ten when this injury occurred. And though there were still two or three years to go before he moved away, I see this as the beginning of the end of our long association. Not the wound itself, or the stitches, but the moment I felt him looking at me and looking away at the same time.

Our closeness was difficult to describe, and even now I'm not sure you could really call it friendship, at least not in the normal sense. Maybe *neighbours* is the better term. Geographically speaking, our houses were close to each other, and we were as neighbourly as any two people can be when they grow up on the concessions around Essex County.

Even if you don't know the place, or have never visited, it's simple enough to understand. Imagine a piece of graph paper laid over top of some of the flattest, most fertile farmland in Canada.

The Ninth on top of the Eighth on top of the Seventh, with the county roads running along the other axis to complete the grid. There were intersections we couldn't avoid, and parallel lines that would never touch. Like in New York City, even though it was nothing like New York City.

Really, the whole county is just a fluke of heat and humidity and some miraculous mixture of nutrients the glacier dropped off in our dirt a million years ago. But that means we can grow anything here. Tomatoes and strawberries and corn and tobacco. Apple orchards and vineyards. People say if you spit your peach pit on the ground, you'll find a tree there next year.

Allan's house was one road up and over from mine. For half the year, when the corn was down, I could see his place clearly from my window, sometimes even the silhouettes moving behind the curtains. But in the spring, as the crops rose up and the workers returned and the whole operation began again, all of that would fill in the space between us. By July, his house, the privacy fence around the pool, the outbuildings, even the three towering curing barns—they would all disappear behind a green density that nothing could penetrate.

Most of the time, especially at school, Allan and I got along well, and we usually found ourselves on the same side of things. Like whenever a partner was needed for group work, we would quickly nod at each other and lock it in before the teacher had even finished her sentence.

But we also competed openly and sometimes viciously with each other. Who could hold their flexed arm hang the longest? Or cover the most distance during the twelve-minute run, or hit the upper limit of push-ups and sits-ups for the Canada Fitness

Test. The nation needed this work. "Excellence" was a red badge and a "Participant" was brown.

Our real rivalries were mostly around individual grades and then overall report card averages. During tests, I was the one who took every minute of the available time. Teachers would have to walk down the aisle and physically rip the papers out of my panicked, still-scribbling hands. But Allan was almost always the first to slowly walk up to the front and submit his work.

He normally sat in front of me, and I'd watch his head bopping up and down as he filled in his multiple-choice boxes, or put the finishing touches on his compare-and-contrast essay, or showed all the work for the long math problem that could only be completed in three or four different stages. He used blue Dippity-do gel to sculpt his hair, tousling it up and over to the side with a precise part, immovable and crunchy, and I could not believe how quickly he could pass through all these evaluations and still come out looking so calm and put together. In the end, when the final grades were released, we'd be separated by one or two points, up or down, but I always felt it took me a lot more effort to arrive at pretty much the same place.

The summer after the trailer incident, Mr. and Mrs. Klassen invited me to go away with Allan for a two-week stay at Camp Calvary. This was a development in my life, a real opening, and I imagined we might be heading towards a different kind of connection—the trusted intimate space reserved only for real best friends.

When the offer was made, I was eager to accept it, but my parents worried about the cost of this adventure, the price *they* would have to pay. The state of my soul, or the potential risk of some deep religious awakening did not seem to enter into their calculations. So when the Klassens revealed that this whole sojourn was already covered, no charge to us at all, my parents said fine and they let me go.

Maybe I wasn't spiritually ready, or maybe I just wasn't paying attention, but I had always heard the word "Calvary" as "Cavalry," and so I had been expecting the camp to be more of a horse-centred, trail-riding, cowboy kind of thing, which it was not. I appreciated the daily campfires, and some of the songs are still with me—"He's got the whole world in his hands"—but after the music ended, it was mostly awkward silence.

I found the sharing circle empty and dull, and nothing real was ever revealed during the nightly "moment of revelation." This was a "devotional time" when we were encouraged to talk about our deepest secrets and tell these strange kids and the even stranger grown-ups who were the counsellors about everything that was really going on "in here."

I remember how one of the counsellors, a younger guy with a spiky, slightly punk haircut and a wooden cross hanging from a piece of leather around his neck, used to touch his own chest, really pressing against his "in here," before leaning forward into the fire circle to hear what we had to say about that same place inside of us.

Allan and I barely spoke the whole time we were there. He had a full set of established friends waiting for him as soon as he got off the bus, and his loyalties were already pledged to other people. We never partnered once during the full two weeks, and we didn't share the same cabin. Sometimes it was as if he barely remembered that we had come here together, or that, in real life, we were from the same place.

He was the first rich person I ever knew. And the Klassens were the first family I ever understood as being fundamentally different from my own. Their tobacco operation was one of the biggest around, and back then everyone was still addicted, so the price and demand for their product was always high and I think they were selling all over the world. When their in-ground swimming pool went in, a custom kidney-shaped job with a slide, I remember my mom talking to my dad. "Well, at least we know the Klassens are doing fine."

Allan's dad was also the first man I ever met who, though he worked as a farmer and was often out in the fields, actually spent most of his day upstairs in his home office. This was a converted bedroom with a real computer and a filing cabinet, a dot matrix printer, and a separate phone line. He was in there all the time, and whenever I went by, it seemed like he was always in the middle of difficult negotiations over something important.

Once, as I was walking down the hall to the bathroom, he looked up from his desk. The phone was pressed into his shoulder and his fingers were on the keyboard and I was framed in the doorway. He gestured a quick hello at me, and smiled, but then someone on the other end must have said something, because his hand flew up to the receiver and he gripped it tight in his fist. A muscle flexed in his face, sharpening his cheekbone.

"I told you: no. And this has got to stop," he said. "It was no last week and I'm saying no right now, and I'm going to say it again if you ever, ever try to bring it back up."

He slammed the receiver down and blew out hard through his nose. Then he noticed me again.

"People," he said, and he shook his head.

—

Mrs. Klassen had a taste for faux French-provincial furniture. Everything was scalloped and curvy and coated with this special pre-yellowed white paint that was pretending to be antique so that it could contrast with the gold flecks of the edging and the metal handles of the cabinet drawers. Their walls were a deep cream colour, and the living room was covered in a lush carpet made of extra-long and extra-thick synthetic fibres that blended three different shades of blue. There was even a special tool for taking care of this carpet, a carpet rake that Mrs. Klassen kept in a nearby closet; every day she would tend to her field, starting on one side and pulling each blade of carpet up to its full height. They also had an oven that was built right into the wall, and they ate off blue earthenware ceramic plates and drank from blue-tinged water glasses with stems.

I could barely understand them. This was during that crucial stage in my life, between the ages of nine and thirteen, when I was fully committed to the classifying business. My goal was simply to sort everybody out and put them in their right slots, but I could never figure out where I belonged relative to Allan Klassen. Or who I was when I was inside his house. Envy was part of it for sure, the purest kind, but more than that, I realize now there was also a different operation going on, a processing I was carrying on all by myself, a deep uncertainty I had to work my way through.

It got strange once with the Sears catalogue. This was maybe in early November, in those first days of the Christmas season, when the *Wish Book* would come crashing into every living room like a brick tossed through the front window. Allan and I played this game where we had to go through the catalogue, every *single* page of this glossy full-colour five-hundred-page book, and we had to pick the one thing we wanted most on each page. There was no skipping allowed, and nothing was too boring or too far away from our interests. Profound questions needed to be confronted and you had to think about things you'd never thought about before. What was my favourite kind of curling iron or crock pot or dehumidifier?

Then pages and pages of jewellery. I couldn't believe how hard they pushed the cubic zirconia. But we had to choose. One of every product. Or usually two: his, then mine. If we had no preference at all, we just went with whatever cost the most.

"Just buy it, then sell it." We agreed.

But the bra and underwear pages were different. Here it was always the same two women and the same two guys, one blond and one brunette, and these models had to run through all the sets. The guys were tanned and strong—but not too strong, you could still imagine yourself like that—and it was boxers or briefs for them. Sometimes undershirts. Two men standing there together, the blond and the brunette in a single shot. Maybe one of them would have his foot up on a chair, or he'd be holding a cup of coffee or a newspaper. For the women it was the same, mostly solid serviceable stuff in beige and white. Nothing frilly.

But then there was one more page, and this was where they put all the red-and-black outfits. Stockings and garter belts. Even the one-piece "Merry Widow" corset. It was Christmastime, and Sears was dropping this into every living room in the country.

"What do you think of this one?" Allan asked me, and he pointed at item 0001-226532-0036 and reached out to touch her stomach. There was a sentence or two of description under the picture. They said it was available in all sizes.

"I don't know," I said. "What do you think?"

"Don't really care," he said, and I think he meant it. "But if you don't want it, then I'm going to take it."

I nodded, and we turned the page and kept going.

—

Allan's bedroom burned an impression into me that I still haven't been able to shake. He had a double bed all to himself, and an actual bedspread that he always kept flat and neat. And then on one wall, he had all his action figures displayed on three different shelves like his room was a curated toy museum.

Han and Luke and Batman and Robin, and dozens of the rubberized WWF guys: the Hulkster, and Mr. Wonderful, and Randy Savage, of course. But also the subtler characters, the wrestlers I truly loved: Jimmy "Superfly" Snuka and Ricky "the Dragon" Steamboat. At our house, between four brothers we had one figure each, that was it, and we used to team them up to stage battles against piles of damp towels—an avalanche!—or alien squids made of bungee cords, or the approaching annihilation of a running vacuum cleaner or a toilet bowl whirlpool. We actually lost our Chewbacca that way, accidentally flushing him down, brown and turd-like. I remember my youngest brother crying with his arm stuffed deep in the bowl, trying to rescue his favourite thing. And then all of us feeling foolish for risking something so precious like that.

In Allan's room, though, there was no need to manufacture some vague threat. His collection included even the bad guys, and every villain you'd ever need was just waiting to be called into whatever story you wanted to make up. Vader and the Emperor's Royal Guards dressed in red, and the entire Legion of Doom. Plus, Nikolai Volkoff, and George "the Animal" Steele, and Big John Studd. The possibilities were almost overwhelming. All the different combinations you could create. You took down the Green Arrow and held him in one hand, and you set him up against King Kong Bundy. Then you smashed them together, whole universes colliding.

Where I lived, in a single-storey bungalow one over and one down from the Klassens, life was not like this, and everything we did felt like a compromise. My father was a grade 4 teacher and my mom drove a school bus and I had to share a room with my closest brother. Across the hall, two more of us were in the same situation. And even in their adult space, down beside the bathroom, I could always hear my parents grappling with each other over money and time.

On Fridays we'd each get fifty cents for allowance and my middle brother would immediately go down to the store, throw the quarters onto the counter, and say: "Show me how much I can get for this."

I think that was the real chasm between us, between me and Allan, the change I felt in the air as soon as I crossed the threshold into their climate-controlled home. In this house, nothing was ever forced, or "the way things have to be." Instead, the whole place was like Allan's room, a carefully selected collection of objects, and making your decision was the only real challenge. Like with the catalogue, all a Klassen had to do was choose. As long as they could accurately identify what it was that they wanted, and pin it down, then they were already well on the way to having it.

—

Mrs. Klassen also tended to another dwelling on the property, a flat building well behind the main house and over beside the curing barns. This was the bunkhouse, a place where the farm's migrant workers lived during the season. There were usually five or six of them, Spanish-speaking men who used to come up every year, probably from Mexico, though I know that wasn't the only country.

There was a connection between the Klassens and the workers that I didn't fully understand, at least not at first. I think the church brought them together. Or it was the church that initiated and then managed the migration process in the early stages, maybe even sponsoring it as a kind of humanitarian aid, before the real seasonal worker program took over and became an official policy of the Canadian government. This cycle had been going on for years, generations probably, but since our family was never directly touched by it, we barely noticed, or we paid attention only during those rare moments when the lives of the migrants spilled over into our own.

Religion had always been mysterious to us. My brothers and I spent our Sunday mornings watching reruns of *The Great Space Coaster*, so we could not understand how two groups of people who barely spoke to each other during the week would, on their only day off, suddenly be able to head off together to attend these services that seemed to run for hours and hours.

"They just have a powerful idea of God over there," my dad said, trying to be respectful.

Setting up the bunkhouse was one of Mrs. Klassen's favourite tasks and she went at it with real pride and ritualized care.

"Where they are from, the men don't have anything," she used to tell us. "So we want them to feel welcome when they're here with us. We want them to feel like they are coming home again for another season."

The bunkhouse was a kind of mini motel operation the Klassens had built out there at the start of their fields, with plywood floors and a metal roof and perfectly squared-off door frames so that each room opened out to the air. The beds had rubberized mattresses and Mrs. Klassen had garbage bags of sheets and pillowcases for each room, and every window had curtains she had cut and sewn by hand. During the winter months, the garbage bags sat heaped on a pallet in their unfinished basement, each one of them labelled with a piece of white masking tape that just said *workers*.

In the early spring, Allan and I would go down to get the bags and bring them up to the main floor or the backyard to air out before everything got set up again. Mrs. Klassen would stick her nose in one of the bags and give it a good sniff and say something like "Not too bad." Then she would delicately take out each sheet and iron it again. And we'd help her make the beds and put the curtains on the white rods and hang them over the nails that had been tacked on either side of the windows.

Then we swept out the place and wiped everything down. We cleaned out the common bathroom and the kitchen the workers would share, and we plugged the fridge back in and tested the kettle and the toaster oven and the two-burner hot plate. There was a beat-up radio and a black-and-white TV, both with creased antennae, but they were still good enough to pick up the CBC and the big American stations. The day before the men arrived, Mrs. Klassen would put a vase of fresh flowers on the kitchen table and stock the shelves with canned soup and saltines, a tin of coffee, and a few snacks just to get them started. Because the men came directly from the airport and had no cars, we also fixed up two or three second-hand bicycles for them to get around with. I even donated one of my old Supercyles, a rusty purple ten-speed with brakes that only worked on the front. We oiled all the chains and made sure the tires were pumped. The men could use these to ride into town to get supplies.

I thought the bunkhouse was just about perfect. When it was all set up, it was much better than the cabins at Calvary, and I remember wishing that I could stay there with the men, or that I could have a place like this just for myself, with my own room and a kitchenette where I could eat when and whatever I wanted.

I wanted to know the men, as much as this was possible, but there were fundamental differences that were not easy to overcome. Language and age, mostly, but we made an honest effort, and I was always trying to close the gap. Some of them were

curious about me too, uncertain about my position in the operation of the Klassen house. Who was I exactly and why was I here,
always hanging around?

"Just a visitor," I'd tell them.

Most of the senior workers spoke very little English, and our
mutual incomprehensibility impressed me like a strange and
massive bird you could only gawk at. The colour, complexity,
and depth of our lack of understanding was stunning, really, even
hilarious sometimes, the way our conversations would stagger
awkwardly through their first few steps before somehow manag-
ing to lift off and carry on in their signature messed-up fashion.
We were always "losing the bus," not missing it, and making little
mistakes around what we could "have" or "be" or "make" or
"do." The subtle distinctions between the things that were closest together were the hardest to clarify.

I remember how Mr. Klassen used to deliver his instructions
one word and one concept at a time.

"*Flower*," he would say, slow and clear, and he'd hold up one of
the blossoms in his hand. Then he'd say, "*Leaf*," and he'd hold that
up too. Then he'd point out to his fields. This was during the important topping-off phase. Every individual plant—it seemed like there
were millions of them—needed to have its blossom removed so that
all the future growth would go straight into the leaves.

"So we all get this now?" he asked, and he flung the blossom
onto the ground and stepped on it, then elevated the leaf above
his head. "Bad and good? Wrong and right?"

Everyone nodded and smiled.

At first, I suspected this was just clever strategy, the men pretending they couldn't understand what Mr. Klassen was saying

at crucial moments. But then I thought about myself—I was always thinking about myself—and it struck me, once more, how disappointing, how embarrassing it was that a person like me, a person with nothing but A+'s in French, still knew almost no Spanish, barely *hola* or *gracias*. And how lonely and useless I would be if the world worked in a different way, and I was the one who had to be dropped off on some back road, in the middle of a field, in a country I had never seen before.

I asked my brother about it once.

"TV should have taught them something, right?" I said. "At least enough English to get by? But no."

He laughed in my face. "Are you really this stupid?"

Then he broke it down. "When those guys are home, they watch their own TV. They have their own shows where everyone speaks Spanish, and all their own songs on Spanish radio. They already have their own everything. Half the freaking world speaks Spanish, idiot."

I hated when this happened—when one of my brothers was right about something, especially when it touched on something important.

He was just lying there on his bed, five feet away from me, staring at the ceiling.

"Don't you get that? Been spending too much time over there with your pal Allan. This is straight work for those guys in the bunks. Come up, get paid, go home. That's it."

Right up until the end, my interactions with the men were generally positive. We waved and smiled to each other, or we looked up at the sky and complained about the weather. Every spring when they came back, I would note how they'd changed, some of them getting a little fatter and slower maybe, or a little greyer. I imagined they did the same with me.

I remember the summer I turned thirteen, after I had gone through a spurt, Edgar, the youngest worker and the nicest guy on the crew, touched the top of his baseball cap and then lifted his hand up higher and higher to show me that he'd noticed how much I had grown. Then he flexed his bicep. His English was the best of the bunch and he often served as our go-between.

"Boy," he said to me. I don't think he ever learned my name. "Almost I don't know you anymore."

Then he pointed at the fields behind the house where the tobacco was coming in. The season for them had barely started and there was nothing really there yet, but in a couple of months, the plants would be way over our heads, more than anyone could handle.

"Watch out, boy." He shook his head. "You go up too quick, soon, maybe boom, we have to take you down."

Edgar swung his arm towards the ground, flicking his wrist at the end of the movement, like cracking a whip. I could picture it exactly, the object he was pretending to hold in his hand. It was a lightweight axe, like a tomahawk with an extra-long handle, and it was the essential tool of the harvest.

When the tobacco was at its peak, the men would each take one of these hatchets and step into the rows and start swinging. Always down and always from the same angle on the right. They would cut the stalks off, almost at the base, and once the plants were separated from the ground, they would bunch them together. To do this, they used hundreds of laths, thin pieces of wood about six feet long, and these were staked into the ground every few steps. Then there was a transferable sharp point that would move from lath to lath, temporarily topping off each stick, so the men could lift each tobacco plant over the spearhead and then viciously shish-kebab the stalk all the way through and down the shaft. Each lath could hold maybe six or seven full-grown plants, maybe fifty pounds' worth, and this would be the unit they loaded onto the trailer, then up into the rafters of the barn to cure.

The men were amazing at this work, stabbing each lath into the ground, then swinging the hatchet and lifting and driving the stalks down and over and through. At this point in the season, they knew they were almost done, so everything accelerated. The pace they could maintain for hours without rest seemed impossible to me. Once they hit their rhythm that was it. Swing and lift and drive it down. Swing and lift and lower. They spaced themselves out evenly and it appeared as if all their actions were choreographed and no motion was wasted. Whole fields could be brought down in a day with barely a leaf lost. Almost like they were part of nature itself, the final stage of the process.

—

My family worked the rows too, but we were always in the corn, and I never really touched tobacco. That crop required experience with the tools, and real skill and strength, so it was reserved mostly for the workers. But almost everything else was available to us. There was an extra-low wage, something below even the minimum, that could be paid to people under the age of sixteen. So for about five years, when we really needed the money, my mom set up a detasselling crew of about thirty kids. It was the four of us, her own children, and then a bunch of others from our classes. She worked out a deal with the school bus company, and for a discounted fee they let her keep it for the summer months. All through July and August, the bus was parked there, right in our driveway.

The fields we worked were mostly leased to the seed companies, and when my mom pulled the bus in at six in the morning, all the plants would still be covered in very heavy dew. For those early hours, we wore garbage bags with holes cut out for our heads and arms, or sometimes we would tie one around our waists like a skirt—anything to keep the wet, sharp leaves of the corn from rebounding and cutting us. There were bad outcomes we were always trying to avoid—rashes and pesticide burns, heatstroke and dehydration, and that nasty bloody kind of chafing that would come if you got too salty around your armpits or your groin.

Hybrid seed corn is planted in rows of three, with a "male" row in the middle and two "female" rows on the outside. Our job was to tug the tassels from thousands of female plants, one after the other, so that the male plants could pollinate them. Though this was repetitive stuff, the pattern in the corn was too random and every tassel was in a slightly different spot, so like the tobacco, there was no machine that could do the job as well as a person.

Most of our best work got done in that first blow, from seven in the morning to around ten, and then at some point in the midmorning everything would suddenly turn inside a tight twenty-minute window. The heat would rise up all the way to ninety-five degrees and the moisture would burn off, and we'd have to tear off our garbage bags and switch to our daylight gear.

Baseball caps and sunglasses, maybe an extra T-shirt tucked under the snapback and hanging over your neck. But nobody ever wore sunscreen—we never even considered it—and some of the burns we got in the early weeks were the bad, blistering kind. Soul-destroying boredom was the other real challenge, and I used to quietly sing songs to myself or count to one thousand again and again to get through the worst hours of the afternoon shift.

Allan never came with us on those detasselling runs, but I still met up with him almost every afternoon at the pool. When the shift was done, and my mom was dropping everybody off, she would stop at the end of his driveway and let me go from there. My bathing suit from the day before would still be hanging there on the back of a chair, and sometimes I'd be so hot, I'd strip off my work clothes right on the deck, super fast, and do the towel trick—wrapping it around my waist while I wriggled out of my underwear and into my shorts. If I was absolutely sure that no one was around, I might even skip the towel.

It was so refreshing to hit the water and feel the day draining out of me, my feet and my fingers loosening up, and the cold taking away the heat.

Allan would hear the splash and he'd stick his head out the window. "Okay, hold on," he'd say. "I'll be down in a sec."

Once, when I had just finished changing, Edgar came through the privacy fence and right onto the deck. He was carrying a large potted plant. It was during that in-between moment before Allan arrived, and I was just standing there in my suit, with the sunburnt lines bright red around my arms and neck, and my chest making a perfect T-shirt of whiteness. Despite the heat,

Edgar was still dressed in long sleeves and jeans and wearing his boots and sunglasses.

When he looked at me, scorched and exposed like that, he shook his head. "What are you, a crazy person?" He waved his hands over my body, and pointed at the bridge of my peeling nose and the rest of my face. Then he reached into his shirt pocket and tossed me a tube of Blistex. He pretended to rub his fingers around his mouth. "Put these on there," he said. "And watch out what you do, boy."

He pointed at the sky. "He is serious business up there."

When I tried to give the Blistex back, he refused to take it.

Then Allan came running through the gate, right past us. He leapt off the edge, as high as he could go, and his cannonball splash exploded up and out.

I was already in my bathing suit, so it didn't matter, but Edgar stared down at his jeans, now soaked below the knee, and his boots, leaking mud onto the deck. He wiped the water off his face.

When Allan surfaced, he was smiling with evil satisfaction, but then he saw Edgar. "Oh hey, man," he said. "Sorry about that. Didn't see you."

"Señor Klassen," Edgar said, and he tipped his ball cap at Allan. Then he took three or four giant steps away from us, trying to touch the deck as little as possible with his boots.

—

My mom ran the entire detasselling operation by herself. And there were many days when she was in the cornfields too, hitting the tassels just like us. I think now about all the things she must have been thinking about. The bus permits and the risk of it, driving in the dark, kids picked up before dawn and dropped off at three thirty, six or seven days a week if needed. Insurance and all the contracts and collecting and paying for what was owed and the inspections for all those different fields. She was always running the numbers and making her decisions. I remember there were policies that some of the other parents didn't appreciate very much. Like the way we never got paid for the time we were eating lunch or for our fifteen-minute breaks in the morning and the afternoon. And the rides out and back from the field were not included. In fact, "transportation fees" were deducted from all our pay envelopes to cover the costs of the bus and the gas and the insurance.

But she was great with the kids, and everybody loved her. And it was great for us too. We were making real money, earning it, and then spending it however we wanted. At our age, nobody else would give us a job, and it felt so good to finally have some power and a bit of control over what we could do with it.

"A little hard work never hurt anybody," she used to say.

Another one of her favourite lines was: "There are people who turn up their sleeves and there are people who turn up their noses and there are people who never turn up at all."

—

The last time I visited the Klassens' house, the harvest was almost complete, and the plants had all been cut and spiked, loaded onto the trailer, and lifted again. Now the tobacco was hanging in tiers from the rafters with their stems to the sky and their leaves reaching for the ground.

There was still one trailer left to unload and it sat parked around the side of the main barn. It was so weighted down the tires were starting to sink into the ground, and soon it would be almost impossible to shift it, but there was no room left in the barn to hang it and they were running out of time. I think Mr. Klassen was working the phones, trying to find another barn in the area that might still have some space.

The men had been going full tilt for about six weeks and I could almost see their bodies fading away, as if they were getting ready to disappear from our lives. Their cheeks were hollow and any extra fat they'd been carrying when they arrived had burned away. Their T-shirts and jeans hung loosely now, and Edgar's ball cap had a new set of salt rings spiralling upwards like the cross-section of a tree.

It was Friday night and the season had been a record-breaking success, and the Klassens were staging their annual celebration out by the barn, just themselves and the workers and a couple of neighbours. The rest of my family had been invited, but they didn't come; they never came to events at the Klassens'.

Allan and I wandered around, listening to the music, but he was barely interested. When I look back, I can see it clearly now. How the summer was the season that separated us. It was the busiest time of the year for my mother and for me, and for so many others. But for Allan it really was time completely off, and his challenge was this vast emptiness in every one of his days. A void that stretched for months, full of hours he could not fill.

The Klassens had music and patio lanterns and a barbecue feast with all the pork chops, burgers, and hot dogs you could eat. There were carrot sticks, and chips and dip, and three kinds of salad, and coolers full of pop. The food was spread out on long tables in front of the barn's main door, and there were a few scattered picnic tables where we were supposed to eat.

But that was not everything. Before the celebrations had really started, Allan and I noticed Mr. Klassen leading all the workers around the corner and past the trailer, to the back wall of the barn, where he had set up a little bar on a folding card table. There were more coolers here, but these were full of cold beer, and there were stacks of paper cups beside several bottles of liquor, and a couple of garbage cans.

Mr. Klassen gathered the men together so they made a circle around him. "Tonight," he said, "everybody can have anything they want. As much as they like."

He waved his hand over the coolers and the table, and I watched as Edgar smiled and spread out a half-dozen paper cups, then splashed hefty shots of tequila into each one.

"Señor Klassen!" he said, and they all raised their glasses and drank in one quick jerking motion. The men grimaced and made contorted faces, but then a second later they all laughed and kind of groaned as they made their way back to the party.

A semi-regular schedule began after that. Every fifteen or twenty minutes, a couple of the men, sometimes with Mr. Klassen, would go around back to the card table for a few minutes. As the trips built up, the men broke down, staggering as they came back around the corner, or rocking from their heels to their toes whenever they tried to stand still.

Once, in between their visits, Allan and I snuck back there ourselves. We poured outrageous amounts. Rum for me, and I think vodka for him. "Señor Klassen," we joked and we pounded it back, but the burning was so horrible we nearly puked, and we had to dive over to the cooler to find some ice cubes to suck on to make the taste go away.

Allan held the almost empty bottle of tequila in his hand and shook his head. "Not going to be a pretty scene around here tomorrow," he said.

When we returned to the party, everyone was just sitting or standing around with their paper plates, staring into the main door of the barn. It was difficult to take it all in, the scale of what we were looking at. The interior of the barn, normally so high and empty, was now filled to the point of structural risk. Its horizontal beams sagged with the weight of the harvest, still heavy with water, and even the walls seemed to heave outward, as if the building itself was telling us it had had enough.

The barbecue roared and somebody lit some citronella torches for the bugs. When it got darker, the automated lights came on: one for the main house, one for the barn, and one for the bunkhouse. The different bulbs made a pattern of intersecting circles on the ground, and Allan and I slid between them, listening to the chatter, a mix of Spanish and English, things we could understand and things we could not.

Around midnight, it was clear the party was almost over.

"That's it for me," Allan yawned. "I think I'm done."

"Me too," I said. "Night."

He turned towards his house, and I turned towards mine.

Then he stopped. "There's no plan, right?" he asked. "We aren't doing anything tomorrow?"

I said no, and he said, "Okay, then. I'll see you when I see you."

He waved at me like this was nothing, and, in that moment, I felt exactly the same way. But it was the last time we ever spoke.

All the other people were going too. I went back briefly to help Mrs. Klassen half-heartedly gather up some of the plates and the cups, but even she gave up.

"Leave it," she told me. "It will still be here in the morning."

The workers trailed away to their bunks, and in the end it was only Edgar and me left. He swayed a little and I thought he was staring at me with an extra intensity. For a second, I felt it, the real connection I hoped we could share, a direct line of transmission I imagined could carry a clear signal between us, even through all of this distortion and interference. I waited in case he needed or wanted anything more from me, but after a minute, he wandered off into the dark like everybody else.

I still had my own plate and cup, and I went around the back to dump them into the garbage. Mr. Klassen was there, sprawled out on a lawn chair, all by himself. He had his hands folded on his chest and his head hung back over the top of the chair, resting against the barn. He was looking up at the sky, the full starless black of it, and his legs were extended and spread wide, like his body was an upside-down Y. One of the coolers was beside the chair, and a bottle was tipped over on the ground by his foot.

I had never seen him like that, so still and completely turned off. I thought he might be sleeping so I tried to be as quiet as

I could as I lowered my plate and cup into the can. Then I began to head home.

I'd taken maybe ten steps before he called out for me. I heard his shoes crunching on the gravel. Slowly at first, then quicker.

He caught up, then passed me on the right and stepped directly in front of me, blocking my path. He was carrying two unopened cans of beer.

Mr. Klassen cracked the first one and handed it to me, then opened his own and took three deep gulps. He mimed the tilting action at me. "Come on," he said. "Give it a try. This is a party. Everyone needs to let go once in a while. You know what I mean?"

I nodded and took a swallow. The way he was talking was out of the ordinary, like this earthy burning fizz taste in my mouth.

"You are always welcome here," he said. "You know that."

"Yes," I said. "Thank you for everything. Thank you for everything all the time, but especially tonight."

"And you can use the pool anytime you like. Even if Allan doesn't want to. You can go in by yourself. I see you sometimes, you know, when I'm up in the office. I can see over the fence. And I like to watch you going in and having fun."

I thought about the angles, the way his office window framed the pool deck so perfectly. I thought of the times I didn't do the towel trick.

"Let me show you something," he said.

And then, in a move I could never have imagined before, he came around beside me and swung his left arm around my shoulder. He still had his beer in his hand, and this banged against my chest as he led me towards the trailer.

He brought me up very close, so that we were both standing by the axle, facing the rows of hanging tobacco. The smell, sweet and vegetal and raw, was so powerful it made my eyes water.

"Do you have any idea," he asked, "how much this is going for right now?"

Standing this close, it was like I was seeing the tobacco for the first time. Cut off at the stalk, speared and stacked and compressed into a massive rolling bale, it did not seem like a plant anymore. Even though it was mostly dark, I could see the veins running through the leaves.

"No," I said. "Maybe a lot?"

He reached out his hand and pushed hard into the green, but the trailer was packed so densely, he could barely penetrate. He shook his head, as though even he couldn't quite comprehend it.

Then, without taking his arm off my shoulder, he drank from the beer in his other hand. He had to almost put me in a headlock to do this.

When he pulled back, the foam was running down his chin.

"Come on now," he said. "Drink up. We are going to celebrate."

I took two more half swallows, but I could barely keep them down. We'd been out here too long.

"You know, Allan is very lucky to have you," he said. "Without you, where would he be? All by himself, up there in his room."

He seemed to really be considering it.

"Sometimes I don't think he appreciates you."

This was something I'd felt every single minute I ever spent around Allan. I was shocked that Mr. Klassen had noticed. You never know who is paying attention.

"But we all need friends, I guess."

"Yes," I said. "I think so."

"What about us?" he asked. "You and me. What do you think? Could we be friends?"

"I don't know," I said. "But thanks again for everything."

I tried to pull away, but his grip was tightening.

"Come on," he said. "We both know this is what you want. I can tell. You just need to let yourself go. Let me show you."

Then it happened all at once.

He dropped his beer, spread his fingers over the back of my head, and pushed my face forward into the tobacco, pinning me against the trailer with his elbow and his knee. He moved so fast, with such clear purpose, I couldn't believe that he'd had this inside of him the whole time—the wires inside his body coiled like that, a pressure so focused—even while he'd been talking and strolling so slowly. I was not prepared for how strong he was.

His mouth was close to my cheek, and though he looked clean-shaven, I could feel the sharp points of his nighttime whiskers pushing through his skin, and I could smell the beer on his breath, mixed with the leaves. To this day, even a whiff from a pipe, or somebody smoking a cigar, will make me want to get as far away as possible. His left hand reached down to fumble with the buckle of his pants while his right hand yanked mine down with sharp tugs. I was desperately trying to hold them up from the front, but he had me flattened against the wall of tobacco, now with his shoulder, and the force was more than I could handle.

But then there was a kind of whistling sound, like a cuckoo clock, and I heard different steps approaching, these ones slow and steady.

"Yoohoo," the whistle said, up and down like that, and Edgar came around the corner.

Mr. Klassen released me and quickly backed away. We had been standing in the space between the trailer and the barn, a gap of maybe fifteen feet, and when he let me go, he moved to the opposite side and pretended that he'd been peeing against the wall of the barn.

Edgar took a few more steps towards us, then stopped.

"Oh hey, boss," he said. "Did not see you there."

Our bodies made a perfect triangle, each of us separated from each other by the same distance.

Edgar smiled and shook his head. "Too much 'Senor Klassen!'" he said. Then he re-enacted the cheersing ceremony with an invisible glass. "Oof," he added, and he chuckled and pounded his temple with his fist and made a sour face, as though tomorrow's hangover was already here.

He was standing slightly sideways to me, and when I looked over, I caught the reflection of the thin silver edge of the tobacco hatchet in his hand, hanging down low almost to his ankle. He held it very tight, close to his leg.

When we finally made direct eye contact, he jerked his head back again.

"Boy?" he said, and then he was right back to the same joking, scolding tone he usually used when we talked. "What are you, a crazy person? Too late. Take my bike, go home."

"Edgar," I said, though I could barely get the word out.

But he was not smiling now, and he seemed much, much older.

"Home," he said again. "*Vamos*."

I ran around the corner and I saw his plan. My bike, our bike, the rusted purple Supercycle, had been rolled up just in front of the barn, and he had put the kickstand down and positioned it so that the front wheel and the handlebars were pointing directly out of here.

As I hopped on the bike, I saw a light shining out of the house from the second floor. Allan was there, perfectly framed behind the glass of his bedroom window. He was staring up and over, not down, and his hardened hair was still perfectly parted and everything behind him was illuminated. You know how it is when the light gets like that. Sometimes the person looking out can't see anything, only the dark, but for the person looking in, every detail is clear.

I was shaking so hard I couldn't get my feet to hit the pedals right. But then I found my balance and pounded away.

I didn't say anything to my parents, and I didn't tell my brothers. I briefly considered calling the police, but I couldn't see any way that their involvement would improve things. I don't think I was sure about what had really happened, or what I had done, or how much it would take to get it undone. Mostly, I was worried about what other people would think if they found out. And I was embarrassed and still terrified.

In the morning, after not sleeping at all, I decided I had to go back for Edgar. I imagined that he needed me.

My brother was still sleeping, five feet away. I watched his chest rising and falling. Maybe he had always been right. This was about money. Money was the only reason Edgar was here.

I took all the cash I had access to. Three brown hundreds from my detasselling envelope and four green twenties from birthday cards.

I waited till around lunch. Then, under the peak of the sun, I asked my mother to drive me over to Allan's.

"What, your legs don't work anymore? You need to be chauffeured around?"

I told her I had twisted my ankle last night and I would only be there for a minute. In and out. Could she just come with me, then wait in the driveway, please?

She drove me back and I went straight to the bunkhouse, but Edgar's room had been completely cleared out and everything smelled of bleach. Two of the other men lingered in their own doorways, farther down the line. They considered me, then shifted their eyes to the ground.

"Edgar?" I said. "Where is Edgar?"

They shook their heads and one of them slammed his door. But the other one came forward. He was fairly new—this was only his second or third season—but I had no idea what his name was.

His eyes were furious, and I knew he believed that if I hadn't been who I was—and where I was, when I was—then none of this would have happened.

"No Edgar," he said. "*Desaparecido.* No more here."

I didn't know what to do. It was only lunchtime, but it seemed like the day was already over. Everything was already over. I stepped back a safe distance, then crouched down and dealt the bills directly onto the ground, spreading them out like I was beginning a game of solitaire. Green, brown, green, brown, green, brown, green.

I didn't know how the international exchange rate worked, but I imagined, or maybe I just hoped, that these pieces of coloured paper might mean something different, something more, if I could only get them safely transported to where they needed to be, thousands of miles away from here.

"You will see him again?" I asked. "When you go home, Edgar will be there? And you can make sure he gets this?"

"Don't know," the man said, but he still approached. He slid the bills together into a neat pile, reassembling the deck, then folded them perfectly in half and tucked the sheath into his shirt pocket.

At that moment, I heard a banging from the side of the bunkhouse, and Mrs. Klassen came around the corner. She was dragging a garden hose in one hand and she had a red scrub bucket in the other. She was breathing hard, and her hair was tied back with an elastic. These were clothes I had never seen her in before: a pair of old sweatpants and a T-shirt that had gone dark under her armpits.

We looked at each other for what felt like a long time. Then she fired a tight stream of water into the bucket, swirled it around the bottom, and flung the mix of wet grit out and away from the bunkhouse. It was a no-nonsense manoeuvre.

"He's gone," she said. The certainty in her voice is what I remember most. "And you cannot be here either."

———

In the days that followed, Allan never called and neither did I.

Then in September, when we returned to school, it was announced that he would not be with us anymore. "Allan Klassen has moved on," the teacher said.

It was some private school in Toronto that took in boarders. None of us had ever heard of it.

—

This all happened a long time ago. I don't live on the concessions anymore, and I never have to go back unless I want to. Almost everything is different now anyway, and I barely recognize the place. Sometimes I even have to drive around the old grid a few times before I can get my bearings back.

Many of the old fields are under glass now. And the hatchets and sharp stakes have mostly been replaced with hydroponic fruit-and-veg outfits that are all computer controlled and pH balanced. Everything grows from a carefully calibrated sponge, and most of the plants never even touch our miraculous soil anymore. The first time I experienced the blinding flash of the new industrial greenhouses around Leamington, miles and miles of nothing but white reflective walls, I thought it was the massive set of a science fiction movie. You should see it at night especially, the way the mostly hollow structures glow from the inside with this pinkish-orange haze. The light is visible for miles, loitering in the sky like a toxic cloud that can never dissipate. Twenty-four hours a day, under the world's biggest magnifying glass, a billion red peppers swell to the perfected size, shape, and colour that is the standard for Canada No. 1-grade produce.

I have never set foot in there, and I've never visited any of the surrounding portable housing units that are usually set up near the greenhouses, but they say that there are currently more than ten thousand migrant workers living here. That's the new scale.

Ten thousand people a season, just for Essex County. It's men and women now, and they come from all over, and sometimes I try to imagine Edgar is still among them, just working for a different operation now, maybe planting and picking and packaging the most recent batch of locally grown cucumbers.

But it's not like that at Allan's. There are no greenhouses there, and no workers anymore. No crops at all, in fact.

This last part is hard to believe, I know, but it is true, and you can ask anybody on the Ninth. A few months after Allan moved away, a routine geological survey was conducted, and they discovered a rich seam of oil under the Klassens' farm. In less than a year, the whole tobacco operation was abandoned and all the gear and the machinery, the trailers and tractors, were auctioned off. The lofted rafters of the curing barns were torn down and the bunkhouse and the Klassens' house with its raked carpets were levelled on the same day. They had to shatter the bottom of the pool before they could fill it in.

A series of wells followed, five of them, evenly spread through the fields, like another set of teeter-totters.

The last time I was home, I went back, one road over and one road up, to the place where I imagined the main barn once stood. It was late summer, and I sat in the tall grass by myself and watched the pumpjack do its work. Patient and consistent, the crank rotated and the head nodded as the well drew up its dark commodity. I found a rhythm inside the movement, the cycle of the machine paired with a sequence of sounds. A hollow knock, then a hiss, then a high-pitched whine, then another hollow knock. It was hypnotic. I laid back and closed my eyes and tried to picture what was really going on under the surface.

I imagined a black lake and I saw myself floating in it. Oil is everything that used to be alive, all the plants and animals of this place but mixed together now and transformed into one solution by heat and time and the immense pressure applied by the weight of the world. I exhaled long and slow and I felt the ground opening up and my body breaking down. Liquid seeped from my tissue, and my arms and legs came apart at the joints, and my brain dissolved and mingled with the remains of a pre-historic seabed. I was raw crude now, drifting towards the valve at the bottom of the well. Then the infinite pipeline took me in and sent me away. It conveyed me across continents and even under the oceans, until I came to understand precisely what I was and how much that was worth.

ONCE REMOVED

SHE DID NOT WANT TO VISIT THE OLD LADY.

Amy studied the stroller, then the bags, then her boyfriend and the baby. She checked her phone: 11:26 a.m. It was time to go. Ninety degrees, ninety per cent humidity, and according to Google, more than an hour each way. There was a colour-coded map that broke it all down: the route they would have to follow and the transfers they needed to make along the way. Each stage had its own icon, like the Olympic events, and all the separate minutes were broken up, then totalled at the end. WALK 10 mins, TRAIN 36 mins, BUS 15 mins, again WALK 9 mins.

Nothing could be worth this much effort on a hot Sunday afternoon.

"Abort mission," she said. "Abort! Just call her up and say we're sorry, but the baby's not right and we can't make it."

She showed Matt the phone. "Are you seeing these numbers? It's a furnace out there."

Matt was holding Ella over his shoulder and doing the humming-and-bouncing trick, trying to lull her into an early nap. A creamy rivulet of drool ran down his spine, but Ella's eyes were already closed and her breathing was slowing down. He nearly had her gone.

He stared at the phone, then at Amy.

"Too late for that now," he said. "Might have had a chance yesterday or last night, but you know she's been baking since six this morning."

He clicked the baby into the stroller and pulled one diaper bag over his shoulder, then tossed the other backpack in Amy's direction.

"Come on. Can't you just picture her? Everything's already set up, and now she's sitting there watching the clock, waiting for us to arrive."

—

Amy remembered a week ago. She should never have picked up that phone. Who else was it going to be making their land line ring?

"So I was thinking next Sunday at one, okay?"

This was before hello. Before anything at all.

"Greet?" Amy had asked. But then she was already on polite autopilot. "Next Sunday? One? I think we can do that, yes. Thanks so much. We'll see you then."

"Good, dear, good. But don't be late, okay? One on the dot. Ring the buzzer."

Then click, then dial tone. Then Amy standing there, the receiver in her hand.

"Is it possible that Greet Walker does not even know who I am?"

She asked this question to the air.

"No," Matt said. "No way." He was categorical about this, which made her feel better. "That would be impossible. Greet Walker *knows* who you are for sure, for sure. It is possible, though, perhaps even likely, that she does not *care* who you are. Don't take it personally. I think it's about exactly the same with me."

Amy stared at the receiver resting in its cradle. She had just completed a short but intense exchange with her grand-aunt-in-law. Her boyfriend's father's mother's oldest sister. *Come on.* Why were they always finding themselves in these sorts of entanglements? It had happened before when he lent money to a second cousin without telling her. His second cousin once removed.

She'd had to look that one up. Online she found a page that explained all the genealogical terminology. In the middle, it had the word SELF written out in big block letters and then everybody else was organized in rows and branches and dotted lines around this one term. The regular stuff was easy enough, parents and grandparents and great-grandparents, brothers and sisters, nieces and nephews, and first cousins on both sides. But after that it got confusing. A second cousin once removed, it turned out, could be a whole generation above or below you. Or you could be twice removed from someone, maybe even three times. Up or down, it didn't matter.

"Like with you and your 'Aunt' Lucille. Or you and 'little Mike,' " Matt explained. One of these people was ancient, the other a child.

She found it weird that he understood her position in the chart better than she did. But he came from a very particular place, Inverness County in Nova Scotia, and everything was different there. Not better or worse, just different.

She'd been born and raised in Southern Ontario, and they'd met in school in Toronto and been together for twelve years. It felt permanent, and they had the baby now, and she had made her adjustments, within reason, to his family's way of doing things. Annual trips back were part of the routine now, and she really did like his parents and the house with the wood stove in the kitchen and how beautiful everything could be in the summers or at Christmastime. The ocean and snow in the hills and all the music. She knew Matt had fantasies of making a grand return in the future, building a new house overlooking the cliff and raising their kids the way he had been raised, but she'd made it clear, early on, that she could never live there full-time.

"It's not for me," she explained.

The families were just too huge and complicated. Matt had five brothers and sisters, some of them married to locals, and there was already a second wave of children starting up and she had a hard time keeping it all straight, where one household ended and the next one began. It seemed like everybody was mixed up in everybody else's business. There was nothing especially wrong with any of them—the whole community was just a little too closely knit for her. And if you were an outsider, it was almost impossible to break through.

The people at his local grocery store, for example, were always asking questions. Not the workers, but customers in the aisle, perfect strangers.

"And who are you, now, dear?" they'd say to her, as if she were only just starting to be herself *now*. "I see you around a lot, but I can't place . . ."

Then the long pause, then, inevitably: "Do you think I would know your mother?"

Or, "Who is your father?"

Or, "Can you explain it? Who would you be, *now*, to me?"

She did not think these were the kinds of things people should ask other people while standing in an aisle beside eight varieties of Shake 'n Bake. The topic never came up when she was pumping gas at the Ultramar on Avenue du Parc, in the middle of a city where everybody else spoke a different language.

"It's not charming, you know. It's just rude." She said this to him once after someone had asked who she "might" be married to. She was not married to anybody. "All I want to do is go in there and buy a six-pack of overpriced cinnamon rolls like the next person. Is that asking too much? They should act like everybody coming through that door is walking straight out of the void. Makes everything much easier."

She didn't understand what people were looking for or what they thought they were finding in these trees. Her mother's side was pure French Canadian, her grandma the oldest of nineteen. She imagined the mathematical possibilities of that one exploding network. Its exponential radiating power. Montreal itself was likely crowded with her people. But please now. You need to be reasonable with these things. At this stage, her own immediate nuclear family felt more like a set of former room-mates, people she used to share an electricity bill with.

When she and Matt had first got the jobs and moved here, to Montreal, for good, it had seemed like they were finally going to get to be alone. Alone together, and starting out on a chic, almost European adventure. Before the baby, they used to eat at a different restaurant almost every week, and on Sundays, they would take the metro to random stations and just pop up wherever they wanted and stroll through all the neighbourhoods they'd never visited before.

But then, maybe eight months in, the first call arrived, the startling ringing, actual bells clanging inside that box on the wall. And they discovered her, or, in Matt's case, rediscovered her. Greet Walker, living on her own in a seniors' building in Notre-Dame-de-Grâce. Their only relative in a city of more than four million people. Or *his* only relative.

"I don't know the whole story," Matt told her, after their first visit. "Some sort of scandal in the fifties or the sixties or what-ever, but she's been living up here by herself forever. We used to stop by whenever we were coming through, maybe once or twice in a decade. But she hasn't changed a bit in all that time. Looks exactly the same today as she did when I was eight. It's like she came through completely untouched. The woman is a force of nature."

Greet Walker. Her boyfriend's father's mother's oldest sister. Amy could put her on the chart now easily enough, but there was something else about this person, a faint whispering sound that Amy imagined she could almost pick up whenever she was around

Greet. And then there were the basic details she could never quite pin down.

Her real name, for example. No one could give a straight answer.

An abbreviated Mar*guerite* or maybe a twisted Mar*garet*? A corruption of Gertrude?

She wondered: Where would you have to start to end up with "Greet" as your final destination?

—

Their apartment was a third-floor walk-up on the Plateau with a metal spiral staircase twisting off the front. The circle was very tight, a double helix of railings, but they had worked out a system. Their stroller was one of those models designed for running, a kind of all-terrain tricycle with knobby tires, but to get it down the stairs, one person had to hold the front wheel, the other the top handle. Then they dangled the contraption over the side as they went down. In the early days, they used to do the stroller first, then climb all the way back up to get the baby and carry her down separately, but they were improving gradually and getting more efficient. Now they just strapped everything into one load at the top. The child, with all her gear, would be hanging there, three storeys up in the air, before they started their descent.

The walk was not as bad as she had expected. There was a bit of a breeze and it felt nice to be out, just the three of them, strolling through the heat and the crowds. They did the wheel-and-handle trick again at the metro turnstiles and then she tilted the stroller backwards and held it in place while they rode down the long de-escalating escalators. She liked the way they didn't have to talk about this process anymore. An obstacle would arrive, and they would simply meet it, each of them moving automatically into position, balancing the load, up and over, and over and out. All you really wanted was somebody else on the other end that you could count on. An actual partner.

As they took their seats, opposite each other, she watched him locking the wheels in place, and then peeking in below the flap to check on the baby and rearrange some of her things.

"I'm sorry," she said. "You know, before at home. I was out of line. I think it's just the heat."

"No problem," he replied, and she knew he meant it.

He tapped the hood of the stroller and smiled. "We got her this far at least. And the rest should be easy now."

Sometimes she admired the way he could let things slide. Sometimes she hated it.

The train started up with its normal *dou-dou-dou* and its lurching. As they moved through the first few stations, she tried to picture exactly where they were right now. And not just relative to the surface of the city, but in the grand scheme of things. Matt closed his eyes and leaned back and let his head bang gently against the window. She saw the stroller in the aisle, then him, then her own reflection in the glass behind. Three people going on a long journey to present a newborn baby to an elderly relative.

There would be food when they got there and something to drink and someone would likely take a picture—the lady holding the child. How many others had done this before, or something very close to this? She imagined all the babies and all the old ladies from the very beginning of the tree all the way down to now.

Maybe that was it. A person just needed to do what a person needed to do. Sometimes, she was almost embarrassed by the profound sense of satisfaction she could derive from completing a single basic task. Paying a bill, or tidying up her desk at work, or arriving at an appointment on time or even, imagine it, five minutes early.

At other times, though, she wanted to flip over the kitchen table with the breakfast dishes still on it and delete every email and burn the whole place down. All this running around trying to please people. For what? Or for who? And what about what she wanted just for herself? She didn't know exactly what that was right now, or where it might fit into the total calculation. But there was a special kind of liquid resentment that could flood her system if she wasn't careful. So bad she tasted it in her own spit, the metallic edge of it, like licking a nine-volt battery.

Some days it was just hard to stay steady and hold it all together. Usually, she saw herself as a forever busy person who always had too much to do and never enough time. But then, suddenly, it could turn around completely, and she'd feel like a person who really had nothing at all, just years stretching on, filled only with these empty performances. One sensation could follow right after the other or, sometimes, both arrived at the same time. Too much, *then* nothing. Or too much *and* nothing.

The train kept starting and stopping. Matt was asleep now, his head rattling off the back wall. She let him go for ten minutes, then kicked his foot. He opened his eyes in a mild panic, but then settled on her.

"Just me," she told him. "Almost our stop."

There was no one else on their bus and somehow they made it to the building with twenty minutes to kill.

"Here?" he asked. "Is this good?" And he pointed at a random bench in a small parkette.

"Good enough," she said.

He unfolded their portable changing station over the graffitied slats and laid the baby down, unsnapped the crotch of her onesie, and brought out the wipes. They had two bottles of pumped breast milk, but they were saving those for later. Amy unbuttoned her shirt and checked the time again. A feed and a blast and a new diaper. Then fresh clothes.

They rang the bell at precisely one and Greet's voice immediately came crackling through the sheet-metal vent of the speaker system.

"I'm watching you on the camera right now," she said. "Go over to the door and hold the handle, and when you hear the buzz sound, pull. Then when you're in, turn around and push it again, good and tight."

"Yes, Greet," Amy said. "We know how it works."

The building had specific rules and a security card system to activate the elevator. You had to wait in the lobby until the person who had invited you came down. Then they would escort you to their door. They had been here two times before and Greet had explained everything the same way, using the same words, both times.

This was the common room over here, and if you wanted to

have a larger event, you could book that space, but this was not a rental place, not a seniors' building the way some people might imagine it. And it certainly was not a long-term care facility or the kind of old folks' home you might read about in the news.

"Even if I was dead, I wouldn't set foot in one of those hell-holes," she'd told them. "These are real *con-do-min-iums*, dear. Just like downtown. We aren't the kind of people who don't know what we're doing."

During their previous two visits, she'd drawn their attention to the quality of the pink industrial carpeting and the fluorescent lighting, and the welcome mats and the sprigs of plastic flowers people had glued to their doors above the peephole.

"Everyone here is fine," she explained. "We know how to plan, how to manage our own money, take care of what needs to be taken care of. We own these homes. This is our property. Nobody else is making our decisions."

The elevator opened, but they did not immediately step in, and Greet did not come out. And this time she was not alone. There was another woman beside her, this one obviously older, much shorter and bent over. She had a walker. There was an awkward, quiet moment as the people inside the elevator studied the people outside.

"That's the one right there," Greet said.

"Okay," the other woman said, and she nodded her head. "Okay."

Amy didn't know who this was, or who they were talking about, but it was only uncomfortable for a second before Greet took over and performed a regular introduction.

"This is my neighbour Regina," she said.

"Just Reggie," the woman said. "Or Reg."

"And this is my nephew Matthew. Well, he's not really my nephew, but we're related, somehow, and this is Amy, and their daughter, Adele. If my calculations are correct, that baby is around four months old, I think."

"Right you are," Matt said, over-cheerful. "Four months." He had an awful fake Cape Breton accent he pulled out for occasions like this.

Amy turned quickly and sent him a message with her mind. *Do not use that voice anymore.*

"Very nice to meet all of you," Reggie said. "Come in, come in."

She gestured them forward, but she didn't move.

In that moment, the elevator seemed like a cave, a cave suspended over a chasm in the middle of the building, held up only by a rope. As Amy stepped across the little gap, she stared at the light coming up from the bottom. *We're just hanging here,* she thought.

They crowded in with the stroller turned sideways and when the doors closed, Greet quickly hit the seven, then the nine.

"Even though Reg and I live on different floors, we are still friends," she explained.

"That's nice," Amy said.

At seven, Greet held the button and Matt and Amy and the stroller popped out to make room as Reg pushed her walker forward and stepped out into the hall.

"So we will see you later?" she said.

"Yes, indeed."

When the doors closed again, Greet turned to the two of

them. "I need you to help her with something after we eat. It won't take long."

"No problem at all," Matt said, but when Greet turned back to the buttons he glanced at Amy and gave her a shrug.

Greet's apartment was the same as before. Mostly beige carpet with a little spot of wooden flooring, a place to take off your shoes, right behind the door. She had a wicker basket there full of hand-knitted slippers. Dozens of pairs, all the same style, with the same tassel on the top, but in different colours of yarn and different sizes, different patterns and different degrees of stretched-outness.

"You'll need a couple of those," she said as she pulled on her own. "When they get the air conditioner rolling, they keep it cold as a crypt in here."

Amy looked at the basket. How many feet had been through here before?

But they each selected a pair. Orange and green for herself. Purple and pink for Matt.

"These are the greatest," Matt said. He wiggled his toes. "Nobody makes slippers like these."

Greet considered him with a serious questioning expression. "What are you talking about? *Everybody* makes slippers just like that. What other way is there to do a slipper?"

Matt had been right. She must have been at it since dawn. The table was set with the good blue-and-white plates and there were water glasses with stems. Amy studied the china cabinet. Such a strange piece of furniture. Behind the glass door she could see all the empty spots, the hooks for the cups and the display ridges where these dishes normally sat, waiting to be called upon.

When was the last time? she wondered. *Us? More than a year ago? Does this woman break these out only for us?* All of it would have to be cleaned by hand once they left. No dishwashers in these units, and the china was probably too delicate anyway.

In the middle of the table, it was exactly what she had imagined that morning: a roasted turkey dinner on a ninety-degree day in July. Amy could tell, just from the smell of the place, that Greet had done everything right and somehow managed to bring it all in on time. Sunday at one. On the dot. She had insisted.

Amy scanned the tiny kitchen. How had this happened?

She knew the stuffing was going to have potatoes in it, the way Matt thought all dressing was supposed to have potatoes. But the potatoes themselves were not going to have any garlic or cheese, or even a little hint of stirred-in sour cream. Boiled carrots sliced into circles, not strips. Broccoli, not asparagus. Everything done exactly the way Matt's family did things.

Greet led them straight from the door to the table.

"I was thinking me here and you there, Matthew, and Amy there, and the baby there."

The table had four places prepared, one on each side of the square.

"Thank you so much for all this, Greet," Matt said. "All the work. But you really shouldn't have. We only wanted to see you. And for you to see the baby. One of us can just hold her while we eat, or we can leave her in the stroller."

He gestured towards the contraption. In Greet's condo, beside the basket of slippers, it looked like some time-travelling pod from the future, all black metal and plastic, taking up the entire front door space.

"She most certainly will not stay in there."

The force of it surprised Amy.

"Look here," Greet said. "I piled up a stack of books, you see, and then we have a nice soft cushion for the top. If we just lock her in, I think we can all have a proper dinner."

On the counter, Amy saw it now: a pile of scarves and lady's kerchiefs, maybe three of them. And one conspicuous piece of old-fashioned rope, coarse, with blue-and-white braiding, like something off a fishing boat. She thought she could see the beginning of what was coming, but she didn't quite believe it.

"I'm sorry," Matt said, "can you say that again? I don't think I understand the plan."

"She can sit right there and eat with the rest of us."

"Where?"

"On the chair, in her spot."

"*Tied* to a chair?" Amy asked.

"Just for dinner."

You think you are in one situation, but then it turns out to be something else. She waited for him to say the words, the polite version of *No fucking way. No way in hell. A pile of books and a piece of rope?* There was a delay and she sent him another message with her mind. *If you don't say it right freaking now, then I am going to say it. But this is your grand-aunt. Your father's whatever whatever. She is yours, right? You should be the one who has to do it.*

But he didn't. The coward. A humid silence hung between them, over the table and the turkey. She could almost reach out and touch her own frustration, swirl it around like steam in the bathroom. Matt looked at her for an awkward moment— *Don't be like this,* she thought—but then he turned away and started up again. The stupid cheerful voice, and the accent.

"Okay then, Greet. We can give that a try for a couple of minutes and see what happens. Never done anything like this before."

"She'll be fine." Greet plowed through. She had the rope ready to go. "We just want to keep her here with us. And this'll get her good and locked in."

Matt took their baby and placed her on the stack of books and held her there while Greet got busy. Breathing only through her nose, she looped the rope around the child's middle, at chest level, and tied an expert knot. Secure, but loose enough too, maybe the same tension as a car seat.

"Matt," Amy said.

But Greet cut in directly, shaking her head at her. "It's nothing. God. If she doesn't like it, if she fusses, then we try something else," she said. "But this way we'll have her here, and we can all be together while we eat."

She folded a green paisley scarf around to hide the rope, but it was not long enough to loop around. "One second," she said. "Can you hold her there for one second?"

Greet went to the closet, a sliding door to the left of the foyer spot, and searched through her hangers. Then she pulled out a black overstuffed suit bag with the Tip Top Tailors logo printed on it. She laid this on the floor and unzipped the front. There were probably five or six men's blazers in there, with shirts inside and creased pants and maybe ten neckties from different eras.

Greet grabbed a handful of ties and came back to the table. Flower patterns from the seventies and skinnier models. She pulled two of these around Ella's body, one at her waist and one under her armpits, then looped them through the vertical slats on the back of the chair and tied two bows.

"Well, she's not going anywhere now," she said, and she smiled.

Ella, the traitor, was loving this. The nap on the train, and the feeding and a fresh diaper. She was in one of those rare windows that came around maybe once a week for them. She cooed comfortably and bathed Greet in these wide, wide smiles as the old woman babbled along.

Then, somehow, for the first time in her life, this was the moment when Ella Beaudoin-MacPherson finally learned to hold up her own head. The muscles in her neck and her shoulders and back tightened and clicked into place, and there she was, sitting up straight and looking her mother straight in the eye from across a table. Even turning her head to see what might be happening over there or over there. They had read in their parenting books that this was already supposed to have happened. It was one of the signposts, a developmental marker they'd been waiting for. Now here she was, past it.

"Will she have some potatoes?" Greet asked, but without waiting for an answer, she plopped a scoop into the middle of Ella's plate.

"No," Amy said. "We're not there yet, no solids."

"Ah come on, now. Anybody can eat a potato," Greet replied. "Really all you need, you know. All we ever had. Goddamn potatoes. When I had to leave, I promised myself I'd never eat another one. But here we are."

Then Greet took her fork—a fork, not a rubberized spoon. A regular fork with steel tines—and she scooped some potato up off the plate and held it in front of Ella's face. "So then how about a little of this?" she said.

"Uh," Matt started.

But of course, Ella leaned forward and gobbled like a pro. One bite, gone, clean tines, no spit, more smiles.

"Good job!" Greet said. "Like a horse, this one. Eats like a horse. Some of them, you know, can be awful picky."

Who are you? Amy thought. *And how would you know anything about what "they" are like?*

She stared at Greet, at Matt, at Ella. They were all smiling, and she thought it again. *Who are any of you?*

She gave up and turned to her own plate. Turkey, even at the right time, even at Christmas, was not her favourite. The bloat to come; she could feel it already. And the pie to top it off, then tea. You could never get these ladies not to put the milk in. There was no such thing as plain tea.

It took probably forty minutes to get through the meal. Then Greet got up and went over to untie Ella.

"I think we can let you go now, little thing. You did such a great job."

She tugged on the bows and they both fell away. The child started to lean forward, but Greet caught her with her palm spread out over the baby's chest. Then Matt scooted over and grabbed her as Greet loosened the rope the rest of the way.

"I didn't think that was going to work," he said.

"Ah, well. Everybody likes to eat, don't they?"

"Yes, but the baby, I mean."

"What? Just like the rest of us in the end."

—

They were drinking their tea, sitting on the sofa and staring out the window, when Greet said: "Do you think maybe we could go see Reggie now?"

Amy had been watching the clock and that's why she noticed it, the precise timing of Greet's question. Just as the words were leaving the older woman's mouth, the second hand was passing over the twelve. Now it was 2 p.m. Right on the dot.

It hit Amy all at once: *We are not the reason we're here.* The baby was in Matt's arms and she considered her as well. *Not you either, buddy.*

She felt slightly disoriented. They were clearly inside of somebody else's plan now, but important details had been withheld, and she had no idea what was coming next.

She looked over at Matt, but again, he did not seem to be catching any of this.

"Okay, then," he said.

Greet stood up quickly and wiped her palms on the front of her dress. Then she went over to a side bedroom and shut the door quickly behind her. When she re-emerged, she was carrying a yellow toolbox with a black handle. The words *Stanley FatMax* were printed on the side. Amy couldn't quite absorb it. Not just the way Greet stood there at her front door, ready to go with the toolbox in her hand, but just the logo itself, the branding. Who on earth, she wondered, had decided that the words Stanley FatMax might encourage somebody to buy something?

"Let's get to it," Greet said.

"Do you need me to carry that?" Matt asked. "Are we doing a job?"

"I guess so, kind of," Greet replied. "Nothing big, though. We just need an extra pair of hands. And somebody a little taller than ourselves."

He offered to take the box again, but she pulled it closer.

"No, no," she said. "I have this. But we should all go together. Reggie will want to see the baby."

And that is how they went, all together, but without the stroller. Amy held the baby, and Greet held the box, and Matt tried to find a spot between them. They went down to seven and knocked on a door that was unmarked by any special decoration, and Reggie opened immediately.

"Sorry I'm a little late," Greet said.

"No problem," Reggie said. "Come on in. Just over here."

This unit had the reverse floor plan to Greet's—the foyer was on the left, the kitchenette on the right—but Reggie still had the same big window and the same place where a couch might go, and the same bedroom off to the side. The main difference was a view looking the other way. And the fact that there was almost nothing left in this apartment. Just boxes and Rubbermaid bins and one dining room chair that matched the set from Greet's place.

"Are you moving?" Matt asked.

"Yes," Reggie said. "Pretty well finished up here. Just a couple things left to go."

"This is what we need you for," Greet said, and she pointed up to the ceiling.

In the middle of the living area, in the spot directly above where a table would have been, there was an ugly medium-sized chandelier with brass accents.

"That belongs to me," Reggie said. "I put it in, and I am going to take it out."

"Don't worry," Greet said. "We have you covered. A couple screws and a little snippy-snip and we'll be done before you know it."

Then she turned to Matt and Amy. "The building just gives out the standard models, cheap bastards. So all we have to do is take this one out and put the old one back up. I was trying to remember how tall you are," Greet said to Matt. "But you're a little shorter than I thought. And we don't have our own ladder, so I hope this will be enough."

She pulled the chair out into the middle of the room, then opened her toolbox and took out an orange cordless drill. "She's all charged up and ready to go," Greet said. "And I think that should be the right Phillips head in there."

"I just cannot have this going to Karen," Reggie said. "Thinks just because she's married to our little Eddie, now she's entitled to anything she wants from everything we have."

Reggie was looking at Amy now, and gesturing towards the chandelier, but talking to the whole room as if everyone in the world knew who Karen was, knew all about her insufferable ways. If Karen thought she was going to walk in here and get that chandelier, *well.*

"You know there are seventy-eight pieces of real crystal up there," Reggie said. "Seventy-eight. Not glass. Real lead crystal. It was a wedding gift. We got it from Henry's grandmother, and we put it up in our home for the first time just after we were married. Then every year in the spring I used to take down every one of those seventy-eight. And I'd set up my vinegar bowl and put on my gloves and away I'd go."

She lifted her fingers off the walker and stood on her own two feet, miming it for them. In one fist, she held the imaginary crystal, while the other hand kept up the furious polishing.

"You should have seen what it used to look like, just after the cleaning, not like now, but when it was perfect. Crazy how pretty I could get it. When we sold the place and came here, it was the only thing I needed to make sure we brought."

Greet pulled a roll of duct tape out of the box. She turned off the light and then placed a strip of tape over the switch.

"Just to be sure," she said. "We don't want anybody to get the hair blown out of their heads during this little operation."

It went just as she'd planned it. Matt stood on the chair and he was just tall enough. He aimed the drill at the screws, and out they came. There was a bracing system to it, more complicated than he first thought it would be, a reinforced cable inside to help bear the weight of the thing as it came down the first few inches.

"I'm not sure about this," he said.

"You'll be fine," Greet told him.

Within twenty minutes, he was untwisting the last orange wire connector and it was done. He had both hands on the base of the chandelier, and he held it by the bar, like some garish brass candelabra.

"Help him, for God's sake," Greet commanded, and she grabbed the baby from Amy and shoved her towards the chair. Then Greet turned to Ella. "Where's my little girl doing her big job?" she said. The older woman's eyes were bright and wide.

Amy went to the middle of the room and raised her hands and Matt lowered the chandelier. She felt the weight transferring. It was heavy, but not quite as heavy as she had anticipated. They moved it together, then rested it on one of the bins.

For a second, on the way down, the light from outside came through the window and caught the bevels in the crystal. Amy had seen something like this before, in a grade-school science class demonstration, the teacher with her prism, breaking up the light. Back then and right now, the room seemed almost to explode. But the colours were more intense than she remembered. They rained down on the beige walls and the carpet and all the people. Red and violet flashing off Matt's face. Green and blue rolling over Reggie and her walker. Orange and yellow for the baby and for Greet. Then changing and changing. All of them rotating around.

It made Amy think of dancing. Dancing with Matt at a real club with a smoke machine and a strobe and the rainbow lasers. Back when his body was still new, when he was skinnier and harder. How much she used to love the techno beats: *utz, utz, utz, utz.*

"Now that piece of junk," Greet said, and she nodded towards the replacement lying on top of one of the bins. It was a basic two-bulber, with only a rounded piece of frosted glass for a shade. It looked like an upside-down boob.

The cheap original went up in less than five minutes, then Matt came down from the chair.

"Can I offer you a cold beer?" Reggie asked before his feet had fully hit the floor.

Amy heard it like a line being recited from a script, like something Reggie had planned for and rehearsed.

"I have six ice-cold beers in my fridge."

"No, thanks," Matt said. He patted his stomach: "I'm about as full as a person can be. We're lucky that old chair could bear my weight after all the turkey Greet stuffed into me."

There was a brief pause, then Greet pointed at three things: the chandelier on the bin, the diminished light in the ceiling, and the clock.

"Didn't I tell you?" she said to Reggie. "What did I say? *We'll be all done by three.* And look now: two forty-five and already in the clear!"

She and Reggie shared an expression that Amy couldn't quite parse. Some mix of pride and relief and achievement. The thing done right. Let the record show.

"Karen is going to be so mad!" Reggie was practically laughing out loud. "Imagine when she sees it. Or when she *doesn't* see it, I guess. Miss *La-Di-Da*."

"You keep your mouth shut," Greet said. "Not a word about this to her or to anybody else. We want it to be a lovely little surprise. She's not going to pull any smart moves on us, is she now?"

Reggie and Greet made Amy think of the schoolyard. Or the way she sometimes still talked with her most trusted friends. The way girls could hate other girls with such perfected mathematical precision. Or hate the old boyfriend, or the asshole ex-husband. How fun that could be and how good it felt: having people so fully on your side of things and so fully against the things you were fully against.

Greet gleefully pulled the tape off the switch and flicked it a couple of times. The measly bulbs went on and they went off.

"How horrible is that?" she asked, holding out her hand. Her joy was almost uncontainable.

"Just perfect," Reggie said. "Now all of you get that back up to your place as quickly as you can."

—

Sometimes, in the middle of a day, you find yourself doing things you never imagined in the morning.

Amy thought this as she stood at the elevator by herself. When the doors opened and there was no one inside, she whispered down the corridor and waved her hand. "Okay. We're clear."

Then her grand-aunt-in-law, Ms. Greet Walker, and Matt, her boyfriend, and Ella, her daughter, emerged from Reggie's place. He was carrying an ugly medium-sized chandelier with brass accents. And the old lady still had the baby.

She held the door open with her foot and quickly checked over her shoulder for any strangers coming from the other direction, then she watched her own people coming closer, one at a time. She thought of the word *caper*. Or maybe *heist*.

At the ninth floor, they peeked into the corridor again, and again there was no one.

"Take her," Greet said, and she handed the baby back to Amy, then scuttled ahead to open the door to her unit. "Now!" she said. And they went together down the hall—Matt and Amy and Ella and the chandelier.

When they were across Greet's threshold, Matt rested the ridiculous thing on the sofa, and Amy clipped Ella back into the stroller.

Amy's heart was beating faster and she couldn't tell exactly what this feeling was: elation, maybe?

Greet was still smiling too, but Matt seemed to be wearing down a bit.

"What the hell are we going to do with this?" he said.

Greet pointed at the closed door of the spare bedroom: "Just put it in there for now, I guess. But there's no rush anymore. We can do it now or wait till you catch your breath. I can put on some fresh tea first if you like. Would anybody like more tea?"

Amy could feel Greet checking them over, evaluating how much strength they had left.

"No, no," Matt said, a little more curt than before. "Whatever you want. Just point us in the right direction."

Greet walked over to the spare room door and opened it partway. "Not a lot of room in here anymore, I'm afraid. We'll have to tilt it to get her through."

Greet went first, then Matt and Amy, angling the chandelier between them.

The room was dark, but not pitch black. The curtains were drawn but some light was still getting through.

"The switch is way over there," Greet said. "I hardly hit it anymore. And I had to tape it up."

Amy could not quite take it all in. There was barely enough room for the three of them to stand. She counted five fully stocked china cabinets. Maybe six. That one over there, with the cutlery cases open and displayed on top, that might be better classified as a buffet. Either way, it was massive. She tried to estimate the combined weight of these pieces, or the amount of solid wood in them. There was no dust and no fingerprints and even the air seemed coated in Windex and Pledge.

She swung her head around and Queen Elizabeth seemed to be studying her from all angles. Her face, the Queen's face, kept aging as she peered out at them from a dozen gold- and silver-edged plates that commemorated the various anniversaries of her rule.

There was a collection of handmade quilts symmetrically displayed on a frame of tiered rungs. And a crude amateur painting of a river going through some trees. And war medals with their velour boxes open. And a taxidermy fox. And a set of souvenir spoons, maybe fifty of them, with ornate ends, mounted to the back wall. The display case featured a detailed wood burning of Niagara Falls, with the words *Maid of the Mist* written above the water in a curling font. On a bookcase, a framed, autographed copy of the classic Maurice Richard photograph, his furious eyes and the ice chips flying behind him, but his handwriting so neat and legible and his number 9 circled.

"How did I never know about this," Matt said quietly. He was still holding the chandelier.

"Ah, it's nothing," Greet said.

Then she seemed to reconsider. "Well, obviously it is something. Lots and lots of something. But in the end, I'm pretty sure, it still adds up to a whole lot of nothing. Just a gigantic headache, honestly. I don't know why I bother."

She seemed to survey the place for the first time. "The trouble is finding good homes for all of it. Or a good home for any of it. Don't know what I'm going to do. For the last little while, I've just been telling everybody who asks, 'No and no and no.' Can't hold any more."

She pointed into the far left corner. "Like those. God, what am I doing?"

On a low table, there were at least sixty paired salt and pepper shakers. Owls and bears dominant, but also a fat Austrian couple in their lederhosen. And soldiers and windmills and insects and toadstools. Then, right at eye level, right beside them: a framed old-fashioned photograph of a little boy wearing shorts and boots but standing in the middle of a frozen pond.

Greet's lips were pursed and she was shaking her head, maybe almost in despair, but then she saw Matt, still holding the chandelier, and she smiled again. "That one is a special case, though, obviously." She reached out and jiggled just one piece of crystal. "This thing. I don't get it at all, but it's so important to her. And I could never deny old Reggie. We have been friends for a very long time."

She tapped a knuckle on the front window of one of the cabinets. "Mostly, they just don't want their things to end up on the street."

Then she thought about it a little more. "Or with the wrong people. A lot of the time, they want to keep it away more than they want to give it away. Like that." She pointed at the chandelier again. "For Reg, any stranger would be better than Karen."

Matt held it up. The thing had no legs and no flat surfaces. You couldn't stand it up and you couldn't lay it down.

"But where?" he asked. "How?"

"Just fill the hole," Greet said. And she tilted her chin towards the ceiling.

Above their heads, it was obvious. The opening in the ceiling and the octagonal bracket exposed and the black and white wires hanging down.

"Last week I put a box on the table there and I stood up to try and get the little guy down, but I barely made it and I wasn't steady at all, and I knew right away I'd never be able to get the big one back up. And there's nobody else anymore. We don't have the people we used to have."

Amy did not like the way that sounded. The word *we* coming out of Greet's mouth. *Who exactly are we talking about now?* she wanted to ask.

Amy remembered the closet by the door, and all the hollow shirts and pants stuffed into the Tip Top Tailor bag, a few decades of bad ties. She thought about the afterlife of objects. All the things that were still here and the people who were not.

She watched Matt stepping up onto the table, trying to bear the weight of just this one inheritance. Greet was following his movements, concentrating hard.

Amy wondered: *How many people did you have to go through before you ended up with us?*

She saw their names at the bottom of a long list. A last resort. And she pictured Greet talking to Reggie just before she made the call. "Maybe," she must have said. "I don't know them very well, but maybe. He's about this tall. And I'll have to cook a turkey, but that's nothing. And do you think you could put some beer in your fridge?"

Matt was trying to hook the support cable into the bracket. "I think I'm going to need you here," he said to Amy. "Can you twist the wires while I hold it up?"

"Yes," she said. And then she was up on the table with him.

To reconnect everything together and tuck it back behind the base plate, Amy had to stand so close to Matt that her hips and her chest pressed up against him. They both had their arms in the air and their shirts rode up so that their stomachs were exposed. She felt the hair around his belly button rubbing up against her bad spot where the extra skin from after the pregnancy was still hanging around. For a second it seemed too intimate, like this was something Greet should not get to see, but when she glanced down, she realized the older woman was focused only on their hands.

When they were nearly done, Greet held up her drill and some longer, sturdier screws. "Now, boom and boom. Right there and right there and I think we nearly have it."

At that moment, in the other room, stuck in her stroller, Ella started to cry. Really cry. Amy couldn't see the baby, but she knew this rising sound. The tone and the pace and the staccato structure of an inconsolable Armageddon-level wailing getting ready to blow. Exhausted and lost, completely spent and blown off course, the girl was done. Her lungs emptied and refilled, gasping and choking.

"I've got her," Greet said. "You finish."

Amy focused on the holes, lined up the screws, and pulled the trigger. The base snugged itself into the ceiling on one side, then the other. She brought her hands down and watched for any give. Then Matt released more cautiously, first one hand, then the other. Everything held. The last part had taken maybe five minutes.

When they dropped their eyes from the ceiling, Greet was

there holding the quieted baby. She was doing the bouncing-and-humming trick, and though Ella's face was blotchy red and bubbles of snot were coming out of both nostrils, she was calming down.

"Now what do you think about *these* people?" Greet asked and she pointed at the two of them standing on the table. "Aren't they smart? Do you think we should keep them around? What would you say to that?"

Amy straightened her shirt and crawled back to the floor and Matt lowered himself too. Then he wedged his way between the tables and pushed some of them aside to get to the opposite wall. He peeled off the duct tape and flicked the switch.

When Amy was a kid she'd thought the word *kaleidoscope* was actually *collide-o-scope*. She thought of this now as she watched the chandelier reigniting in the dark and turning everything else back on. The colours broke open again and all this new light reflected off the old glass and the silver and the polished wood. They stood there under it for a little while, but nobody said anything.

Then Matt did something he shouldn't have done. Rather than just leave it alone, leave it on, he started violently flicking the switch too many times. The strobing hurt everyone's eyes and the baby didn't like it and Amy was irritated by the overproud way he was standing there with his legs too far apart. He got like that whenever he did anything. And the tone of his voice, so ridiculous.

"Just checking for sparks, ma'am," he said. "We need to make sure that connection is safe. But I think I got it. You should be all set now."

"Yes, yes," Greet said, clearly unimpressed. Then she turned and spoke directly to Ella. "We never would have thought of that one without *him*, would we? Who do you think put the tape there in the first place? How could the old lady ever manage without her big strong man?"

The snark of it surprised them, the overreach.

Matt raised his eyebrows at Amy, but Greet was rolling now.

"God," she said. "Sometimes I almost forget what it's like to be with them when they're this age."

At first, Amy thought she was talking about the baby, but Greet was gesturing at Matt.

"I know, I know. Some of them are great, especially for these sorts of things. A little carrying and a little lifting here and there, but some of them. Jesus. They *can* take it out of you. You know what I mean?"

"Yes," Amy said, so quickly it surprised her.

She tried to match her face to the face Greet was making. She had read in a magazine that matching your facial expression to another person's was the best way to demonstrate a fundamental agreement. That and repeating back to them the last three words they had just said. But she could not read Greet's tone at this moment. Some of that was meant to be funny, she thought, some of this is a joke, but most of it is not.

"You know all about what happened to me, of course," Greet said. She was still bouncing the baby. "Back then. Why I had to leave home and come way out here in the first place. You've heard all about that, I'm sure."

Amy locked eyes with Greet. "No," she said. And suddenly she was very serious. "Nobody has ever told me anything."

Greet snorted through her nose and appeared to consider it, Amy's pure ignorance. Then she looked over at Matt, still standing by the switch. Him, too. Perfectly clueless. There were things that could be said right now. Amy tried to imagine the words that Greet Walker might be able to wedge into this space.

There was a long pause as the older woman seemed to think it all the way through, but then she shook her head and shrugged her shoulders.

"Ah, it doesn't matter now, I suppose," she said. "Look around." She gestured at the plates, and Rocket Richard, and the Queen and the fox. "Such a fuss," she said. "For me and everyone else. You wouldn't believe it. The things we had to come through. People wouldn't give me the time of day sixty years ago, now they leave me with all this."

She reached over to straighten the picture of the little boy in his shorts standing on the ice. "But then I guess they're all dead now."

This came out in a flat, matter-of-fact tone. "My parents and the nuns and my brothers and my sisters and all the people who used to gossip and the others who used to listen. But not a soul has anything to say about me anymore. It's like none of it ever happened."

She turned to Ella and opened her eyes extra wide and made the contorted smiley expression again. Then she repeated the same words into the baby's sodden face, but this time in that singsong, up-and-down fake-happy tone that adults only use when they are talking to infants.

"Like none of it ever happened."

She handed the child back to Amy and turned her face away from them.

Amy stared at Matt, standing there across the room, then at Ella, then at Greet.

Matt took a step towards them, but as he did, Greet sucked in a deep breath, just through her nose, and she straightened up to her full height.

"No," she said, and she clapped her hands twice and rubbed them together. Then she plowed on. "Now is everyone here absolutely sure they don't need anything else to eat?"

—

Ella pushed harder into Amy's chest. The smell coming off this kid, from both ends. Chunks of vomited potato stuck to the front of her nice dress, and a dark liquid starting to leak out of her diaper. Greet's clothes were a mess, too.

"Gonna need a full reset here, I think," Amy said. "Diaper bag, under the stroller."

"Ok," Matt replied, and he passed by them and out of the room without saying anything more.

Greet watched him go, then lifted her eyes to the chandelier. Amy followed her gaze. It was hideous. They both shook their heads and chuckled.

She heard Matt rummaging through their things in the other room.

"I found it," he said, eventually. "Don't worry!"

"Good job," Amy replied.

She rolled her eyes at Greet, and the old woman smiled, and Amy imagined telling Ella this story in twenty years.

"She's not alive anymore, your great-grand-aunt, and you can't remember any of this, but once she tied you to a chair and stuffed you with potatoes until you puked. And your dad and I, we stole this ugly chandelier and we drilled it into her ceiling. And then . . . And then I don't know what happened to everyone after that."

In this daydream, or whatever it was, this vision, the adult Ella, or maybe it was a teenage Ella, Amy couldn't be sure—she only caught a glimpse of her long hair and her long legs—but this girl, she turned away from her mother and towards something else, her own device, shining in her palm. Not a phone, but maybe the thing that comes after phones. Just a ball of light, drawing her in.

Amy saw them only for a second, herself and this older girl, talking, but then she lost it, and it was late afternoon in Montreal again. Ninety degrees and ninety per cent humidity and it was still going to take more than an hour to get home.

She knew they had to leave as soon as possible. The routine was shattered and the rest of this day lost. Underground, the air would be stale and hot, and Ella would likely fall asleep again, at the perfectly wrong time, as they rattled through the tunnels. Then at three in the morning, she and Matt would be at it again. The same ancient struggle, trying to get a child to go down while all her energy headed in the opposite direction. She saw these next hours so clearly, it was like they had already happened.

But maybe it did not have to go that way. And maybe everything that was coming could also wait. Amy felt Ella's breathing, and her pulse, slowing down. Her own body followed. She considered the buffet and the china cabinets, taken apart in other places and carried here to be reassembled. All their crowded drawers and shelves. Outside, the day faded, but in this small room, under the fixture, she felt a bright stillness descending, as though the distant past was surging forward while the future rushed back. Ella and Amy and Greet. They paused, alone and together, surrounded by hoarded riches. All the things other people had loved, and all the things they did not want other people to have.

THE CLOSING DATE

THIS HAPPENED NOT FAR FROM WHERE WE ARE NOW.
The Bide-a-While is still there, but after the whole story came
out—or at least most of it—they had to change the name. The
place closed down for a couple of months before they staged a
grand reopening as part of the larger Sleep Station chain. Now
the sign is blue instead of faded orange and there are stars and
moons around the words, but from the outside it looks like business is about the same. Long-haul truckers and highway work
crews, salespeople with samples in their trunks, contractors on
short-term jobs that have to be done right here and right now.
All the in-betweeners. They still need beds and places to rest
while they are away from home, and this building, with its single
storey of a dozen rooms in a line, can still do the job. Sheets and
towels are changed and there is a person who will pluck unsightly
hairs from the white porcelain sinks. Lipstick smudges and grey
fingerprints get wiped away and all the glasses are rinsed and
rewrapped in a special wax paper that promises sterilizing power.

Wastebaskets are emptied, carpets vacuumed, tiny soaps and shampoos restocked. The stubborn red circle of rust around the bathtub drain is scrubbed and scrubbed again, and the last guest leaves just before the next guest arrives. Different credit cards are swiped. A rotating privacy is what they offer, and we were part of the cycle for a little while. In and then out.

We only chose it because it was cheap—half the cost of the Super 8 or the Quality Suites down the street—and because it was exactly where we needed it to be: a block and a half away from the house we had just bought, the permanent home we moved into two days later. This was back at the very start of everything for us, when this was a new city and we'd just got the new jobs and almost a new set of lives, or at least a new strategy for the way things were going to run. Our daughter, Lila, was four years old, and Maddy was seven months along and nearly ready to go with Henry. Between these two pregnancies we'd been through one very sad, very late miscarriage, and we were trying to be extra careful this time. No sudden swervings, no need to strain unnecessarily. We made a detailed but not very ambitious plan for our move and the Bide-a-While was part of it. Two double beds, a mini-fridge, and a coffee maker for sixty-three dollars a night. After the Montreal apartment had been cleared, we were going to drive to Halifax and stay in the motel for a couple of nights while we waited for the movers to arrive. Our closing date, the moment of the official transfer, had been locked in for months and June 1 was stamped on all our documents; but before the house came to us, we were going to pause and reset. We wanted to be ready for the change.

I think everyone has spent at least one night in a place like the Bide-a-While. When we were kids, my parents used to search for exactly this sort of no-nonsense operation, a bargain option with drive-up parking where they might let us swim in an unsupervised, unheated outdoor pool, twenty feet away from the trucks and the steady stream of highway traffic. There were five children in our family, and my parents would ask for adjoining rooms whenever they could find them. The owner would hand over this strange extra key—usually chained to an oversized block of wood or a thick piece of plastic—and we'd get to turn the secret silver doorknobs and then run back and forth through that opening in the wall that normally stays sealed to most people.

The paired rooms were identical but opposite, mirror images of each other, with two double beds on each side pushed up against the shared wall. We'd burn off whatever energy we had left jumping across the chasm from one bed to the next and our parents would let us stay up late to watch weird, sometimes Québécois, TV in one room while they went across to the other side together. If it had been a hot day on the road, they might bring along a six-pack of beer or a bottle of wine and maybe a bag of chips or some leftover pizza. After half an hour, one of them would get up and quietly close the door on us. I remember the click. Then we'd be alone, together with just ourselves but separated from them for maybe an hour before they'd come back and we'd split up again along different lines. A couple of us would sleep on one side with Mom and the rest in the next room with Dad.

When the news story came out, pictures of the motel were everywhere. Police cars and flashing lights, caution tape and pylons, men in hazmat suits entering and leaving the mobile forensic unit. It was what you'd expect. Half a dozen satellite trucks pulled into the parking lot for that first week and a line of journalists, beautiful people of different races, all with perfect hair, reported live for the national and international feeds. The story ran in the papers for months, almost a full year. For a little while, it felt like the whole world was paying attention—nothing animates us more than a dramatic loss of life. But for Maddy and me, maybe only for us, it seemed that all this reporting—the whole brouhaha with the cables and the lights and the reflectors and the split-screen analyses—was missing the real point. At breakfast in the new house, over cereal and orange juice, we'd watch the shows and read the papers, consuming something much higher than the recommended daily allowance for safe exposure to this kind of content. Slowly, we became familiar, almost intimately familiar, with the photographs of the victims and the accounts of their sad backgrounds. And we began to shake our heads at the editorials, the in-depth think pieces, and the searches for explanation. Sometimes, it even felt insulting, as though all these strangers were talking about something they knew nothing about. Over the course of that public year, day by day, as the story came out, we took possession of it, or maybe it took possession of us, and though we never wanted these roles, we were transformed into characters with lines and clear parts to play in the plot. Like wandering through a thick fog, the world's bantering about the Bide-a-While surrounded us entirely and we were forced to breathe it in.

The murderer, as everybody now knows, ran a plumbing business. His truck was already there, parked in front of room 107, when we pulled in the first time. On the driver's side door, he had a rectangular magnetic sign that could be slapped on or peeled off as the truck moved between its work life and its other life—a basic clip-art icon of a bucket catching five separate drops. Underneath it said *Want it done right? Call 902-555-0111.*

We didn't see him at all that evening as we unloaded our bags and our toaster and kettle, our box of road food. Juice and bananas and bread and marble cheese and crackers. This was the night of May 30. It is important to keep the dates right and put everything in proper order. The next day was the thirty-first. At about eight thirty in the morning we left our rooms at the same time: Maddy and Lila and the murderer and me. We closed our side-by-side doors and entered the outside world at the same moment.

We had errands to run and forms that needed to be filled out. Insurance, and a trip to the lawyer's office and then back to the realtor again, and the utilities and the phone. The list was complicated and disjointed—more work than we had expected—but every task needed to have a line put through it.

Maddy was hustling Lila towards the back seat on the passenger side. I can still see it: her perfect four-year-old's summer clothes, the dress and the sandals and the floppy hat. There were yellow straps tied in bows over her shoulders and a little puff, an extra floof of air in the skirt that made it stick out away from her legs. The shoes had red flowers on the toes and her skin was still shining and greasy from the heavy dose of spray-on sunscreen we had just applied.

As Maddy and Lila passed by the murderer, he smiled and held out his right hand for a high-five and Lila gave it to him hard. He wore blue cargo pants with lots of pockets and a grey tucked-in shirt with more pockets on the chest. In his left hand, I remember, he was carrying some needle-nose pliers and he had a roll of duct tape hanging on his wrist like a bracelet. Again, this was the morning of the thirty-first. We've been over it. There was nothing strange about the way he walked out of that room, nothing strange about the way he handled these objects. He opened his door and threw the tools into the cab, and when he turned around he saw Lila still standing there holding out her hand for the return high-five. He gave it back right away.

"Have a good one, Little Miss Lady," he said. And he looked over the roof of the car and smiled at me and nodded. I unlocked my door and pushed the automatic button that opened up everything else on the other side. I watched him bring his right hand up to his nose and sniff. Then he made a big show of pulling his head back quickly and pretending that the powerful tropical sunscreen scent burned his nostrils.

"Ho-lee coconut!" he said, and he waved his palm in front of his face.

Lila laughed in that delighted way that only she could do. She had that laugh for only a couple of months, maybe between the middle part of three and the first part of four—I don't think anybody can hold it much longer than that—but it was there in that moment, and she was giving it up for the murderer. A pure expression of wonder, straight-up happy surprise, untouched by thought. I loved that laugh so much, loved that she could bring up that sound without any effort.

"Sill-lee," she decided. Then: "Silly, silly, silly," with a little music in it. She pointed directly at him, then directly at me. "Silly man," she told me.

"Why thank you very much," he said, and he gave her a little bow.

He pulled a pair of sunglasses off the visor and put them on. They had reflective lenses and when he turned to us the second time, I saw myself and Maddy and Lila held there on the surface of the glass.

"Have a good one, buddy," he said to me. "You sticking around for another night? Not checking out?"

I nodded and he gestured at our doors.

"Maybe we'll see you later on."

We got in and turned our keys. The engines started and I waved at him to go first. He gave me a thumbs-up, then quickly stuck his tongue out at Lila as he pulled away.

—

Before we found this house, Maddy and I used to stay up very late searching for it, a laptop balanced between us in bed. We'd scroll through the real-estate listings, dozens of them, maybe a hundred a night, and we got very good at moving the Earth with our little gloved computer hand. Lila would go down around seven thirty and not long after that, we'd construct a fortress of propped-up pillows and then take turns gently swirling our middle fingers on the mouse pad. The computer rested between us, pressing down into both our laps, and I remember the sensation of the heat from the battery and the buzz of the processor vibrating against my cock. The machine kept kicking off this steady blue glow as the pictures flashed in front of us and sometimes, when the backgrounds changed from light to dark, I caught a glimpse of our faces held close together and staring back out of the screen. Our expressions were blank and our mouths hung halfway open, but our eyes were sharp and intensely focused. We looked like different people—strangers lit up by this weird trancelike concentration, a couple who did not know they were being observed.

"This one," Maddy would say and she'd dart at a listing quickly and click and point and click and point again. The tip of her tongue slid across her top lip as she thought through the possibilities, and I could hear the fluctuations in her breathing, the catches and releases, surges and disappointments. At this stage, she could do things to me without even trying. And her hair was down, and she was wearing her glasses and her pyjama bottoms and the tank top I liked. But it wasn't the right time.

"Focus," she said, and she tapped the screen.

It was always summer in the photographs—full trees and lush gardens—and there were never any people in the frame, even when we switched to the Google Earth Street View. I think there must have been an algorithm, an elegant bit of code, that was inserted into the images to automatically subtract the pedestrians or the dogs or anything that might distract a buyer. We made our way, block by block, one house at a time, moving through the abandoned streets. Eventually, we got a feel for the market and a sense for the cost of things. The numbers we read seemed to make a pattern we thought we could understand and we started to see everything as a mathematical equation, a pure exchange. The places we didn't like were ugly or insanely over-priced—only a fool would live there—and all the places we wanted were special and unique, good long-term investments, and certainly worth the enormous debt we would have to take on to get started. We were looking for something on the edge, a hidden gem that did not announce itself in an obvious way, a house with a special potential that not everyone would be able to see.

—

When the detectives came to us the first time, they had all their facts in order. Credit card receipts and the motel's log and the one long-distance call we made to Maddy's parents, even the Interac transactions for the groceries and for the thirty dollars in gas I'd bought from the station down the road. This was incontrovertible evidence, rock-solid data drawn from the permanent digital record of the world. The information plotted us into a single square on a tight piece of graph paper. Our location at that particular time and in that particular space could not be negotiated retroactively.

"Think back," one of them said to us. This was the younger one, closer to us in age, and more eager and friendly in that strategic way that police sometimes seem friendly. The older one was quiet and more tired, but he did his best to make us feel at ease while his yellow notepad and his digital recorder rested on our kitchen table. We served them cups of tea and all four of us went through it two or three more times while the kids were upstairs sleeping. Later, they would take us to the police station and ask us to make separate statements in separate rooms.

"I want you to put yourself back there on May the thirty-first and I want you to visualize exactly what you were doing and exactly what was happening around you. Tell us everything you saw, everything you can remember. The smallest detail may turn out to be important."

The older man rolled his pencil between his thumb and his middle finger. The red light on the recorder stayed solid.

"Just look at it again," the younger one added. "The thing we need may not have been something you noticed the first time around."

—

The weather records backed up all our statements. May 31 was unseasonably warm, ten degrees hotter than the day before and well above thirty by the late afternoon. Our errands with the car had gone poorly—we couldn't find anything on the first try—and Lila had been straining in the back seat, sweating and complaining for hours. We needed supplies and a break so it was decided that I would drop the girls off at the room and then run to the grocery store. It was four o'clock when we pulled into the motel parking lot. And when we opened the door to our room, a wave of heavy, almost boiling air rolled out and washed over us.

"Great," Maddy said. Her face was pale and I could see a thin purple vein throbbing at her temple. Her hair was matted on the back of her neck.

"Too hot," Lila declared. "Too, too hot."

There was no air conditioning, but we flipped on the overhead fan and opened the back windows and popped the screen on the door to create some feeling of circulation. After five minutes, the air was moving, but things were not better.

"Let me run and get some stuff," I said. "At least some drinks and a bag of ice and some more bananas. If it doesn't improve in the next hour, we'll find somewhere else for tonight."

"Okay," Maddy said. "Go, but be back here as quick as possible. I don't think I can handle much more."

It did not feel like an important decision at the time. There were things that had to be done, and I don't think I gave it a second thought as I turned around and left all of them there in that burning room with the fan circling over their heads.

In the end, it took me forty-five minutes, maybe almost an hour, but everything changed while I was away. When I came back through the door, the handles of five plastic bags digging into my fingers, I found the murderer sitting on our bed and only Lila left in the room. Her hair was still wet, and swooped back with leave-in conditioner, and she was bouncing up and down on the other bed in just her underwear. The murderer watched her calmly and I did not think—I still don't think—there was anything out of the ordinary in the way he looked at her. Lila was chanting, "Up-and-down-and-up-and-down-and-up-and-down."

She had a jumbo Mr. Freeze in her hand, a thick blue tube of softening ice, and the murderer was sucking on an orange one, holding it at the bottom with one hand and sliding the cold syrup up to his mouth with the other. As Lila bit and chewed through the slush, the melting dye leaked out of her mouth in two parallel rivulets that dribbled down her chin, her neck, and her stomach before coming together again to pool in her belly button. She saw me and smiled and her teeth were almost purple. The murderer waved his finger at me, his only acknowledgment.

"Hello?" I called out. "Is anybody else home around here?" I was louder than I needed to be.

The bathroom door opened and Maddy came out. She was wearing one of my old T-shirts with just a towel wrapped around her waist. The slit came almost all the way to the top, and her breasts and her stomach pushed against the yellow fabric of the shirt. Her hair was slicked back like Lila's and her face was bright and beautiful, recovered and cool and happy again. She had her own half-eaten Mr. Freeze, a red one, and her mouth was dark at the corners too.

She pointed at the murderer. "Thank God for this guy," she said, and then she rushed through her story.

"So we're sitting here after you left and I'm thinking, 'Maybe a shower, a cool shower, to blow the stink off.' But then, of course, the taps aren't working right and all we have is hot, scalding hot, like it's pouring right out of the kettle—there's no cold anywhere." She shook her head and waved her hand back into the flawed bathroom. "So I go to the front desk, but there's only a kid there and he doesn't know anything and he says he has to call the manager and that we will probably have to wait till tomorrow. So I'm completely losing it now, and I'm walking back to this freaking hole and I can't believe this is happening and then I see the truck parked right there and I think, 'What the hell?' So I knock on the door and this is Mark and I tell him our situation and he says, 'No problem at all.' Out he comes and he's got all the right tools in the truck and he opens that little hatch under the taps and two seconds later the hot is off and we have complete cold and it's perfect. Not glacier cold, but just cold enough. So I give Lila a quick little hair wash and a cool-down rinse, and when we come out of the bathroom Mark is back at the door, but he's gone across the street to the store to get everybody Mr. Freezes. I ask him if he'll watch Lila just for a second so that I can get my turn in the shower and he says no problem again, and now you're back and that's it. Here we all are."

Lila kept bouncing up and down through all this, nodding her head, and the murderer did the same. They all had their own different-coloured Mr. Freezes and they were all happy.

I thanked him. "What do we owe you?" I said. "For the rush job, you know? These kinds of things, last-minute rescues, don't normally come cheap."

"Come on," he said, but his hands were waving me away. "What are you talking about? It was nothing at all. Took less than two minutes."

He leaned back on the bed, resting on his elbows, and he looked up at the ceiling fan, watching the blades make their whirling cuts through the air. There was a bit of a breeze coming down now and I could see his hair rustling where it stuck out from beneath his cap.

"Whenever you need the hot back, just give me a shout, and I'll crank her back open." He jutted his chin to the wall that separated our rooms and he laughed. "If we could open that door there, I wouldn't even need to go outside. Could slip in here and get it done while you were sleeping."

I hadn't noticed it before—probably because I wasn't looking—but there it was, painted the same colour as the wall to make it blend in, just a few feet over from the headboard. I doubted it had been touched in years. Families were smaller now and people did not travel in large groups anymore. Maybe for baseball tournaments, I thought. A baseball team might need to open that door.

"Just give me the signal and I'll leap into action," he said. "On call twenty-four-seven for all your emergency needs."

This was the evening of the thirty-first. If what they say in the papers and on the news shows is true—and there is nothing, nothing anywhere, to suggest the reports aren't completely accurate—then he killed the second person, the young man, that night. Probably just a few hours after his time with us and likely less than ten feet away. He went from our taps and our Mr. Freezes, our bed and our fan, and he walked out of our room and on to his next task. The woman had been days earlier, before we arrived, but there is a chance—more than a chance—that the man was already there with us, waiting on the other side while Mark sipped from a cold tube of sugar water wilting in his hands.

Of course, none of this was known to us at the time. None of it mattered. We had other things, our own things, to concentrate on, more lists to go through. It took more than a year, almost two, before we started to understand what had happened.

—

The first time we saw this house, we recognized it. It felt as though the place was sending out a signal that only we could pick up. Maddy wrote an email at 1:27 a.m. and we called first thing the next day to set up the viewing and the inspection. The realtor picked us up at the airport in a silver SUV and it took her maybe thirty seconds to figure us out. She took one look at our shoes and our sunglasses and our haircuts.

"Yes," she said. "This should work out well. This is exactly the kind of place that people like you like."

High ceilings, chunky mouldings, heavy iron grates and radiators, plaster and lath, all of it left alone and original. An old fireplace, untouched for a hundred years but still working, grandfathered in before the rules and the building codes changed. We liked that there had been no renovations and nobody had messed with anything or tried to put in a propane insert.

"These old character places are great," the realtor said, "as long as you're okay with the problems."

The inspector showed us cracks in the foundation and pointed out actual seashells that were decomposing in the sandy cement of the basement walls. The roof was definitely going to need money sometime in the next five years, and the chimney was going to be trouble of course, but we blurred through all that and worked it out. We had the higher numbers from Toronto and Vancouver and Ottawa popping in our heads and we allowed ourselves to use the word "bargain" before we sank ourselves in completely.

"I'm going to put my chair right here," Maddy said, and she pointed to the tight corner, the nook she still loves. "And my lamp will fit there and this will be my reading spot. Close enough to the fire, but not too close. I can rest a cup of tea on this ledge."

I put my palm flat against the old wall like I could send and receive messages that way. "Does this mean it's done?" I asked. "We're done?"

Maddy looked at me and her eyes were wide and she was smiling hard. "Yes," she said, and she gave three quick crisp claps. "Yes, for sure, for sure. This is exactly who I want us to be."

The job and the new city and one girl and a lost baby but another on the way. Now the house. Forces were working on us and there were chain reactions that couldn't be controlled. Our bodies were a mess of tissue and bone and nerve endings, primal synapses and firing receptors. Sporadic electrical currents surged in our brains and all the signals were confusing. They say there is a name for this experience, a raw nesting instinct that hits during pregnancy and drives us forward to prepare for a new life. Maybe that explains it, or at least it provides a little cover. Maybe we were in a phase, a period of extreme change like puberty or menopause, and maybe hormones and chemistry did have something to do with it, but I'm not sure. I don't think it was limited to the female body because I felt it just as hard as Maddy. I was caught up in the same way. I wanted this house, this particular house, and I wanted to put it in order. Long before we actually owned the place, when it was still the property of other people, an older couple, I used to dream of what I would do to it. Rip out the hedge in the front and rebuild the back deck and repaint every single surface on the inside.

—

In those first days, the murderer was the only person we knew in the whole city, our only connection. When we saw his face on the news, almost two years later, it was like one of our old friends, someone we'd lost touch with, had received a community service award and he was finally getting the recognition he deserved.

"Is that Mark?" I asked Maddy, and I pointed at the TV. The soon-to-be famous mug shot was there filling the screen, the one where his lips are slightly parted and his eyebrows are pushed down low and there's a little V in his forehead that gives him the appearance of a person who is thinking very hard about something. "The plumber from the motel, you remember? The guy who fixed the taps. Is that our Mark?"

It turned out that Mark actually was his real name and that he was a kind of missing piece, the essential link no one had noticed before. Like a constellation or one of those tricky 3-D optical illusions where an image slowly emerges from the background only after you learn how to squint the right way, Mark was a pattern, a web of connections and contradictions that had always been there but could only be seen once they were pointed out. The distances he had travelled seemed too far and there was no consistency in the people or the places or the timing or the way things unfolded.

In TV interviews, expert criminologists tried to hide their admiration as they marvelled at the perfected randomness of his actions. They called his behaviour "highly irregular," but I am not sure about that. I think he had a system, a special way of studying his people that let him see something in them, a common aloneness, or a sort of halo that glowed around them and guided him or pulled him forward to seek out those who moved through the world like he did. People who shared that kind of isolation and did not have other people looking for them or asking questions about where they had gone. Every one of his victims' case files was considered cold before his arrest reactivated them. A woman from northern New Brunswick, five years earlier, then later, another young man from around Kenora, Ontario. A slightly older lady from a completely francophone community in the Gaspésie.

The girl from Esquimalt, practically downtown Victoria, was the first. I think of her often, stepping out of that place with all the gardens and the flowers and the massive British Columbian trees that seem like they could hide dinosaurs. Nine victims in total. Everybody knows the grid of their stacked photographs. Three on top of three on top of three. It was on all the front pages.

They stopped him in Saskatchewan. A female hitchhiker felt a current coming off him and declined the ride, then wrote down his licence plate and called it in with a description of the truck and driver. The plate was stolen and the police immediately pinged the GPS in her cellphone—the chip inside a cellphone is what ended it all. They pulled him over, fifty clicks down the road, half an hour later. When he stepped out of the truck, he calmly told them everything: names and dates, specific sites where the remains would be found. He pulled the little lever and leaned the seat of the cab forward. He had an array of different licence plates and a set of different magnets for the truck all with the same slogan, the same bucket, the same drops, but different area codes. He could pass for local almost anywhere.

He told them about a motel in Nova Scotia where they still rented rooms by the week or the month. He'd been there almost two years ago at the end of May. There had been a woman in her early forties and then a man in his twenties, eight days apart. They were the fourth and fifth. He was precise about his practice and spoke calmly about ether and duct tape and bungee cords and plastic. He told them what he knew about chemical solvents and drain cleaners and active bacteria. They passed a purple light over his tools and it all showed through. The police cars and the rolling lab pulled into the motel parking lot hours later. A team of expert dogs trained for exactly this task went into the woods outside of town and came back in twenty minutes. It was easy for them to follow the smell when they were pointed in the right direction. In the past, they'd found mass graves that were more than sixty years old. No amount of scrubbing or time could hide these facts from them. The satellite trucks and the cameras appeared the next morning.

—

Right after this, just when the news broke and the crews were on the scene and the details were still unclear, a woman I barely recognized—somebody from way up the street—knocked on our door. It was in the evening and Henry and Lila were almost ready for bed. The woman had a tea light burning in a small mason jar and she held her hand over the top, gently, as if the flickering glass held a butterfly she'd just caught and did not want to lose.

"Yes?" I said.

"My name is Candace," she announced, very formally, like a grade-school kid. "The people from the community are organizing a little memorial and we thought you might want to know that, this evening, there will be a candlelight vigil for that poor couple from the motel."

It was clear she'd said these lines many times before, on all the other porches before this one.

"Nothing fancy, just candles and flowers, I think. Some people are going to sing or play music, but you are welcome to just stand silently. We are going to start in about half an hour."

"Thank you," I said.

Nothing like this had ever happened to me before and I didn't think the opportunity would come again. The invitation was made and there must have been a chance, a second, when I could have accepted, when I could have been taken in and carried along, but I did not go for it. A clinical part of my mind, something colder than it should be, kicked in, and I spoke when it would have been better to stay quiet.

"Oh, I didn't think they were a couple," I told her. I can imagine my blank face staring into hers. "My wife and I, we heard, we thought it was two separate things, two separate incidents. We heard that the people didn't know each other at all, maybe didn't even see each other. We didn't think there was any connection."

An expression of deep confusion rose up in Candace's eyes and flexed across her forehead, then switched to anger, almost disgust.

She said the word: "Incident?" And then she snapped.

"Well, they are a couple to me. And lots of people around here like to think of them like that, together and not alone."

She turned and stamped away from me. The candle almost went out.

—

This is the rest of it. This is what really happened, just to us, on May 31, the night before our closing, the night before we moved into our home, the night he killed the young man and made him disappear.

On our side of the wall in the Bide-a-While motel, we had bought a big cheap bottle of sparkling wine—1.5 litres of not-champagne—and we put it in a wastepaper basket and poured half a bag of ice over it and let it stand for an hour. Then we packed up the rest of our loose stuff and we loaded the car. By eight o'clock we were set and everybody was in their sleeping gear and it was my turn to take the freezing shower. When the water first hit my chest, I gasped hard and I felt all the air leaving my lungs, but then I gradually got used to it and I relaxed a little and I was able to at least rub the small soap over my body and rinse. It took maybe five minutes and then I dried off and pulled on the last of my fresh underwear and my final clean T-shirt. I tousled my hair a bit and walked into the bedroom.

Maddy was waiting on the other side of the door and she held up both her hands, palms flat and right in my face. She pointed at our daughter and made the shush sign with her fingers on her lips.

Lila was face up in the middle of the other bed, arms and legs starfished beneath one thin blanket. Her eyes were closed and her breathing was deep and regular and steady.

"How did that happen?" I whispered. "Tranquilizer dart? Something in her milk?"

"Nope," Maddy said, and she smiled. "Nothing we did, just a summertime miracle."

She raised Lila's limp wrist about a foot off the mattress and let it fall back down. Nothing registered. The girl's breathing kept that steady pace.

"Gone," I said. "Completely gone. Unbelievable."

We were both clean and we smelled better than we normally do. There was an opening.

I kissed Maddy and when our tongues touched, both our mouths were wetter than usual. She put her hand on the back of my head and her fingers went through my hair directly to my skin. She stroked the ridge where the back of my skull tapered into my neck.

We took the basket and quietly went back into the bathroom and closed the door almost all the way, leaving only a crack. There was barely enough space to stand so I put the basket in the tub and stepped in there with it. When I pulled it out, the bottle was wet and sweaty and I undid the tinfoil and twisted out the little wire. I shook it a bit, enough so that the white plastic cork flew with a muted pop and hit the ceiling before rattling back down. The fizzy wine ran up and over my hands and we quickly poured it into the bathroom glasses.

"Here we go," I said, and I held out my glass for her to clink. "To this."

"Yes, to all of it." Maddy laughed and she gestured to the lump of wet towels shoved into the corner behind the door.

We clinked and downed our glasses in one gulp and then quickly refilled. This was the first drink Maddy'd had since we found out about the baby, but we were only a few weeks away now.

"One more of these is not going to hurt anybody," she said, and she drank again.

I stepped out of the tub, and we sat there on the edge and leaned into each other. Our pinky toes touched. The carbonation made a mist in the glasses and everything in the room was so tight and so compressed, you could almost hear every separate bubble bursting.

I put my hand on the soft inside of her thigh and my thumb grazed the edge of her underwear. We stayed still and silent for about thirty seconds, thinking it through, and then we went for it for real, kissing again, with more urgency. There was no room and we had to spin around and almost elbow each other in the face as we tried to get our shirts off. As we kissed, she ran her fingers down the bones of my spine and then brought her hand around so her palm was flat on my chest. I pulled her in close and hard.

It had been a long, long time for us. Every little flutter with Henry's pregnancy worried us and all we wanted to do was get through unscathed. Again: there were mysterious chemicals flowing through our bodies and our brains, especially in these final stages, and we believed we were maintaining a delicate balance that shouldn't be fooled with. There were names, medical terms, in our *What to Expect When You're Expecting* book that we read out loud like an incantation though we did not understand what they meant. It seemed that no one knew for sure. *Progesterone, oxytocin, prostaglandins.* Nothing behaved in the same way every time and there were reactions and counter-reactions that could only be experienced and never explained or predicted. The doctors had told us that our miscarriage was nobody's fault and that nothing had gone wrong. A completely natural occurrence, they said, a thing that happened all the time, but we did not feel that way. Now though, at last, in that tight bathroom, it was all coming back and it felt as though everything inside us was working correctly again, accelerating and rushing down the right channels.

"Maybe just a lick," she whispered. "Please."

We took the last good towel from off the rack and put it down on the toilet seat. Maddy spread her legs, resting one foot on the edge of the tub and the other in the dip of the gooseneck from the tiny sink. She braced her hands against the wall and I went down on her. My left hand rested on her stomach or touched her full hard breasts, while the fingers of my right hand went in and out of her, very gently, and my tongue stayed on the right spot.

"Slow," she breathed. "Go slow."

It was perfect. I could feel her tensing and relaxing, tensing and relaxing, and blowing out these long, long breaths.

"Good," she said. "So good."

After a few minutes she put her hands in my hair and pushed me back. I moved to the left instead of the right and I smashed my head on the stainless-steel leg that propped up the sink. She wanted me to stand up, but when I backed against the bathroom door, one of the hooks jabbed me in the neck.

"Smooth," she said, and she laughed.

"This is not easy," I said.

"Now you," she said. She put the towel on the floor in front of me and knelt down on it. Then she pulled my shorts down and put my cock in her mouth and worked the shaft with her hand. Too many things were happening at the same time, the new and the familiar were mixing and I couldn't keep up. I looked around the room and imagined our next move. Us trying to do it standing up in the tub or somehow crouching down into this square of tile. The angles were all bad and I didn't think any of them would work. We were running out of space and time.

"Out there?" I whispered. "Do you want to try out there?"

I opened the door. The curtains to the parking lot were still half open and a beam of end-of-day light fell directly onto Lila's face, but she didn't stir. I took two or three quick strides across the room and pulled the velour drapes closed so that they only glowed around the edges.

Maddy was on her back on the other bed, on top of the blankets. We would have no cover if Lila woke up.

"Are you sure?" I asked.

"Yes," she said. "We're fine. Come on. Right now."

At the start, all I could do was concentrate on Lila, watching her for any sign of movement, and imagining how Maddy and I could maybe both roll off the side and duck down behind the bed if we needed to. I did not want to get caught in the act by our four-year-old and end up leaving some scarring image that would be seared into her brain forever.

Then we shifted positions, standing up with Maddy pushed against the wall. The pressure was rising and the pace increased. From that stage on, I closed off and I can't clearly remember exactly what happened or the order things followed. Something gave way inside of me, in both of us, and after months and months of stillness it felt like we were moving again, doing what we were supposed to.

"On top," she said after a little bit. "I want to be on top."

I rolled over onto the bed and she straddled my legs and put her hand on the headboard. She pushed down very hard, and I pressed back up against her. We were getting closer and there was no concern for Henry anymore. Raw sounds were coming out of us, and we were saying words we would not normally use. I could just vaguely sense that things were getting louder and louder, more insistent, but it didn't matter and I didn't care. Maddy's eyes were closed and she was grinding down and sliding herself back and forth very fast. The headboard was making steady regular contact with the wall and the lamp shades were quivering. We both had all our weight, all our strength, behind every movement.

I was breathing hard, and my legs were actually starting to burn. I was just going to say something when we heard these three booming knocks coming from the other side of the wall. The spacing was even and methodical, like a machine with a two-second delay between each movement. A thud and then a thud and then a thud. We glanced at each other, both our chests expanding and contracting. We were close, but we could not be sure if this sound came in response to what we were doing or if it was entirely its own action. The two were likely connected— the timing too close—but we could not be certain.

Though the sound originated at a level close to our heads, it also seemed like the blows were coming through the whole wall, rippling outward like a wave, or the concussive vibration you feel in your chest after a firework explodes, or when they are excavating for a new underground parking garage in your neighbourhood. It did not seem like this could be the work of a single hand or a forearm or a shoulder hitting just one spot. I looked up and I thought I could see a crack opening up and moving down through the plaster. Then, across the room, in the dresser mirror, I saw the two of us, still going furiously. Her back pounding down, my hips rising up. We were seven months pregnant with our second child, but he was not in the world yet. In the other bed, Lila, his big sister, did not stir. The noise from us and the noise from the other side did not reach her.

I stared into Maddy's face and our eyes locked, and she shook her head. Before I could say anything, she reached down and clamped one hand over my mouth. Our rhythm increased.

"Do not stop," she said.

We carried through all the way to the end. Our actions did not trigger the premature birth of our son, and our daughter slept through to the morning and no other sound ever rose from the other side. No secret doorknobs were turned and no phones ever rang and no inquiries were ever made. The night of May 31 faded quickly and completely into our shared past, and on the morning of June 1, our new lives began and continued on for almost two years.

But then the TV showed his picture and the other story—the bigger one that includes us all—began. The detectives visited our house and sat around the kitchen table while the children slept upstairs. We told them almost everything—our move, our plan for the Bide-a-While, the house, the sunscreen, the taps, and the Mr. Freezes—but we kept the last part only for ourselves and we never gave that away. The booming signal sounding in the night—the message that may have been sent directly to us, or maybe through us into the larger world—did not make it into the official record. When they took us to the station, Maddy and

I gave our independent statements and we delivered them in different rooms to different officers, but when they were placed side by side, they matched up perfectly, the same gaps inserted into the same spaces. For years, we have kept that sound to ourselves and it is not something we share with other people.

I think we think about it a lot, though. Or maybe we just hear it repeating in our memories. The sound and our silence are combined now, and the consequences of our choices—the things we did or did not do—are hard to understand even though I have tried to run through all the other possible scenarios. Perhaps our quietness saved our lives and saved the lives of our children. Perhaps we were spared. Or perhaps the noises we made and the noises we heard but never reported led directly to fatal outcomes for other people living their lives in other places. Perhaps we are partly responsible for what happened to them. Perhaps the possibilities the murderer was trying to open up on his side of the wall shut down other possibilities in our lives. It is hard to know. I cannot tell where privacy ends and the rest of the world begins.

But I know that our lives are much quieter now and that there is an almost museum-quality stillness in our house. Maddy gets tired much earlier than before and we go to bed at different times, and we do not share the same computer anymore. Now we have our own devices, iPhones with always expanding screens and better picture quality, and we use these to usher ourselves into our own unique versions of sleep. It does not feel strange. The kids go down and we clean up the kitchen together and we take our showers. Then we sit together for a couple of minutes before she says, "I think I'll go up now," and we kiss and say good night. In separate rooms, on separate floors, we choose the shows we want to watch and these pictures and these sounds bring us a specific comfort. They help us rest. Somehow, she still loves her *Forensic Files*, the deep, soothing voice of the narrator, and she is always willing to go back and revisit her favourite episodes of *True Crime*, or *Grand Design*, or *House Hunters International*. There are likely others now, new series she is streaming by herself, but I am not entirely sure. I never ask, and I know she is not interested in the wins or losses of my sports teams, or wherever I go when the West Coast games are over. When I come upon her in bed, I try not to disturb her, or even touch her body, as I take my place beside her. We both have to be ready to go in the morning.

This house has served us well and we have never regretted our choice. All the old character is still there in the walls and the mouldings, and the place is filled with the histories and the trace elements of all the other people who came through before we arrived. Some nights when I have the fire going, I can imagine them, the former residents, generations of strangers, staring into this exact same spot and stretching out their hands towards the heat and the light. But they are all gone and this place belongs only to us now. We have made it the way it is. Our particular actions and inactions, our most intimate longings and revulsions, have come together to form a daily domestic shape that only we designed and only we can fully recognize.

But I go back sometimes, and I see us at the beginning of everything. We are together in the mirror of the motel bedroom, and we are seven months pregnant with Henry and we cannot help ourselves. Then the wall dissolves and now I am looking down from above and I can see him too, just a few feet away, his hand in the air, waiting for a sign. At other times I picture him sitting silently in his own kind of quiet room, the cell where they keep him today. I imagine a cot and some books and the stainless-steel toilet. Mark and I and Maddy and Lila and Henry: we do not know where we are in the arc of our lives—old or young, safe or exposed, closer to the beginning or the end, brushing up against death or far away from it. We do not know if the decisive moment has arrived or if it is yet to come. Led only by what we desire, we go out into the world, and we make our way. And then we sleep, each of us in temporary bedrooms that will one day be occupied by other people.

ACKNOWLEDGMENTS

Earlier versions of some of these stories appeared in the following literary magazines or anthologies: "The Dead Want," originally titled "Cousins," appeared in *iLit Modern Morsels: Selections of Canadian Poetry and Short Fiction*, published by McGraw Hill Ryerson in 2012. "The Closing Date" was featured in *Sex and Death*, an anthology edited by Sarah Hall and Peter Hobbs, and published by Faber & Faber and House of Anansi Press in 2016. "Lagomorph" appeared in *Granta 141* (2018) and later in *The O Henry Prize Stories 100th Anniversary Edition 2019*. Special thanks to Madeleine Thien, Catherine Leroux, Rosalind Porter, Luke Neima, and Laura Furman for the support they gave to this piece. "What exactly do you think you're looking at?" appeared in French translation as "La Parade des Assumption Purple Raiders" in *A Dark Thread: Des Nouvelles Noires Inspirées Par Les Photographies De Henry Wessel*. This special edition text was published by MACK Books and La Maison Européenne de la Photographie in 2019.

I want to thank Mark McCain and the Artworkers Retirement Society for introducing me to the photography of Henry Wessel and inviting me to be part of the *Henry Wessel: A Dark Thread* exhibition, mounted at La Maison Européenne de la Photographie in 2019. The images that inspired "What exactly do you think you're looking at?"—*Pasadena, California*, 1974 and *Pasadena, California*, 1975—were featured in that show in Paris.

While I worked on these stories, my writing was supported at different times by grants from the Canada Council for the Arts and Arts Nova Scotia. I also want to give special thanks to Marilyn Smulders, the kind and dynamic leader of the Writers' Federation of Nova Scotia. Harold Hoefle, my first reader, again scribbled his way over all my pages. I will always look up to him as a model of generosity and care.

My agents, Jenny Hewson, Susan Golomb, and Francesca Davies, provided me with excellent counsel every step of the way. Jonathan Galassi, Jared Bland, Robin Robertson, Ana Fletcher, and Željka Marošević all stepped in to support these stories at crucial stages of their development, and I feel honoured to work with such an excellent team of publishers. Jennifer Griffiths elegantly designed the collection, inside and out, and the text was expertly cared for by copy editors and proofreaders Shaun Oakey and Melanie Little.

In the end, though, as it has so many times before, this book will always come back to Anita Chong, my trusted editor at McClelland & Stewart. Her sharp eye, her carefully tuned ear, and her profound sense of story guided me in all the most important ways. I owe her so much.

Every member, young and old, of my large and very wise family contributed to this book in some way, and I will always hold fast to the people of Curry Avenue and R.R. # 1 Inverness. I am also thankful to the Garrett and Morrison clans, and the McCormacks, and the Ryalls. During the rougher periods in the production of this collection, I was often sheltered by my friends: Doug Vincent, in his mode, and Michel Ducharme, *toujours dans le monde imaginaire*, and Danny MacLennan, Jennifer VanderBurgh, Crystal Bona, Owen Gottschalk, Rich Tremain, Mark Kiteley, Drew MacAulay, Jason Petro, Seán Kennedy, Kris Bertin, Anakana Schofield, and Andrew Steeves.

Our children, Evelyn, John Robert, and Frances, make everything in this world better. Sometimes, especially when we are doing nothing, I just want to hang out here, like this, forever. Appreciation also to Panda and Gunther, the animals who put us in our place and know us better than we think.

Finally, Crystal Garrett, a survivor, and the strongest person I know. All the best lines in here were sharpened by her wit and her journalist's desire for clarity. She came out of nowhere and, this is true, decades ago, she really did randomly pick the seat next to mine at the start of what was supposed to be a long bus trip. Since then, it has been a million miles, rattling along, but we are still in those seats, and I could not be more grateful for the company.